'I *knew* you were going to be trouble,' Keir went on. 'You've been in the country less than twenty-four hours, and already it's been nothing but a catalogue of disasters!'

'I would never have come if I'd known it was going to be like this.' Poppy's green eyes flashed dangerously. 'I'm here to take photographs, not take part in some survival course. I've hardly had any sleep, I've been jolted over a poor excuse for a road, I haven't had anything to eat except for a doughnut—well, two doughnuts—and I'm fed up with being lectured by a cross between Dr Livingstone and Hitler! You may think I'm a problem, but has it occurred to you that you're not exactly the best thing that's ever happened to me either?'

Keir's hands gripped the steering wheel convulsively. 'I'm a very peaceful man normally, but if anyone could drive me to violence, it would be you! And another thing! How dare you tell Henri you were my wife? The blood runs cold at the mere thought of being married to you!'

WEST AFRICA

THE TROUBLE WITH LOVE

BY

JESSICA HART

MILLS & BOON LIMITED
ETON HOUSE   18-24 PARADISE ROAD
RICHMOND   SURREY   TW9 1SR

*First published in Great Britain 1991
by Mills & Boon Limited*

© Jessica Hart 1991

*Australian copyright 1991
Philippine copyright 1991
This edition 1991*

ISBN 0 263 77358 2

*Set in Times Roman 11 on 12 pt.
01-9112-48137 C*

Made and printed in Great Britain

CHAPTER ONE

POPPY stood by the baggage carousel, fanning herself with her passport. The hot West African night was suffocating after the air-conditioned plane, and she wiped her upper lip with a weary hand. What a trip! A seven-hour delay at Gatwick, a missed connection, and now, to cap it all, it looked as if her bags had gone astray.

As if to confirm her fears, the carousel shuddered to a halt. It was empty apart from a box and battered suitcase with a sad, unwanted look. Poppy sympathised as she squinted through the glass barrier at the seething mass of jabbering, gesticulating humanity waiting for the arrivals, her eyes searching the crowd for anyone who looked as if he might be Dr Keir Traherne.

'The expedition leader is a bit of a boffin, I gather,' Don Jones had said. 'Apparently he's very well-known in scientific circles. I've sent a telex telling him when you're arriving, so he should meet you at Douala.' Poppy had nodded absently, fingering her ticket and wondering if she had done the right thing in agreeing to go to Cameroon to take photographs for Thorpe Halliwell, the computer company who were sponsoring a scientific project to conserve the rain forest. Now she wished she had paid more attention. She should at least have asked what Dr Traherne looked like.

Suddenly she caught sight of a vague-looking man of about sixty who was peering through the barrier into the hall. Poppy brightened. That must be Dr Traherne. He looked an absolute poppet—a storybook scientific genius type with rumpled hair and absent-minded expression.

Hoisting her precious camera bag on to her shoulder, she started towards the exit. Her bags were obviously not coming, so she had better introduce herself to Dr Traherne before he gave her up for lost. She emerged into the hubbub, a little over-whelmed by the press of people, and began to push her way through the crowds towards him. Poor old Dr Traherne must have been waiting ages and would no doubt be delighted to see her at last.

'Penelope Sharp?'

The deep voice, clipped with impatience, came from behind her. Poppy glanced round, puzzled, and found herself staring into a pair of ice-grey eyes that stopped her in her tracks with an odd catch of breath. The heat and chaos of the airport seemed to drop away as she looked. They really were re-markable eyes, cold and light, and somehow start-ling against a deep tan and dark, almost black lashes.

With a start, Poppy realised that she was staring ridiculously. The noise and colour around her clicked back into place and she shook herself free of those eyes to focus normally. An austere-faced man of thirty-five or so was frowning down at her.

'Ye-es?' she said cautiously. The man looked distinctly unfriendly. He had an aggressively de-termined chin and the compact physique of a man used to living rough. Rather ordinary-looking really; she could see that now. She had been misled by the jolting impact of his eyes; now he seemed merely dark and neat in his crisp white short-sleeved shirt and khaki trousers. He carried a leather briefcase under one arm.

Obviously an efficient type, Poppy thought, subconsciously noting that his high cheekbones gave his face a faintly exotic look that sat uneasily with the impression of curt command. Suddenly she found herself looking once more into eyes that were as warm and inviting as glacial streams, and blushed hotly as she realised that the man was unamused by her inspection.

'I'm Keir Traherne.'

Poppy's mouth fell open in ludicrous astonishment. '*You're* Dr Traherne? But——' She cast a longing glance at the older man, who was now waving through the glass at someone in the baggage hall, and then looked back at Keir Traherne. This Dr Traherne was most definitely *not* a poppet, and clearly not in the least bit delighted to see her.

'What on earth's the matter?' he demanded, dark brows drawing together at her surprised expression.

'I thought you were a scientist,' she blurted out before she could stop herself.

'I am. Not all scientists wear white coats and carry their degrees around with them, so you'll just have to take my word for it, I'm afraid,' Keir replied caustically.

Poppy flushed. 'I know that, of course. You're just not . . . what I was expecting.'

'Well, if it's any comfort, you're not what I was expecting either. You appear to be the only unaccompanied white woman on the plane, otherwise I would never have approached you.'

Keir folded his arms and looked Poppy up and down, taking in the mop of unruly brown curls, the ingenuous green eyes and wide mouth that tilted up at the corners as if in a permanent smile. She was a tall girl, and naturally slim, with a kind of coltish grace, but under his scrutiny she was aware only of what a mess she looked. She had been wearing these clothes for two days now, and now they clung to her in the sticky heat like crumpled rags. She didn't notice that her loose blue shirt was buttoned up askew, but Keir did. He sighed.

'I understood that Thorpe Halliwell were sending out a professional freelance photographer.'

'That's what I am.' Poppy lifted her chin proudly.

'You'll forgive me if I say you don't look it.'

'At least I carry my cameras around with me,' she retorted, patting her camera bag. She met his eyes defiantly, prepared for their unnerving coldness this time. 'Otherwise, you'll just have to take my word for it, I'm afraid.'

Her mimicry was uncomfortably accurate, and his face darkened. 'I'm taking Thorpe Halliwell's word, not yours. I told them I wouldn't have any women on the project, but they insisted that you came.'

'No women? Why on earth not?'

'Largely because in my experience women are nothing but a bloody nuisance out in the field. I've deliberately kept this an all-male project, as I haven't any time to waste dealing with anyone who can't keep up physically and mentally, or who isn't prepared to get their hands dirty. We've also got only a very limited time to get all the work done, and the last thing the men need is women around distracting them!' He broke off and glowered at her. 'What's so funny?'

Poppy choked back a giggle. 'I'm terribly sorry, it's just . . . well, I didn't think that anyone actually said things like that any more!'

'Are you trying to be funny, Miss Sharp?' Keir asked ominously.

'I rather thought you were,' Poppy confessed.

'I've got better things to do than stand around entertaining you,' he snapped, 'and the sooner you realise that this project is a very serious business, the better it will be.'

So much for a warm welcome! Poppy suppressed a sigh. 'But if you're so anti women, why didn't you say so?'

'I tried to, but Thorpe Halliwell were insistent that you came as a condition of their sponsorship, and, lord knows, I'm in no position to turn down the kind of sponsorship they're offering. According to Don Jones, you're a remarkable photographer.' Judging by the disparaging look he gave her, Keir obviously found it hard to believe.

'I'll do my best,' Poppy said demurely, secretly pleased by Don Jones's recommendation.

'Have you got any experience of rain forest photography?' he asked in a cold voice.

'No—I'm afraid my most exotic experience to date has been a day-trip to Boulogne.'

'Well, I hope to heaven you know what you're doing.'

His determinedly unwelcoming attitude was forcing Poppy on to the defensive, but she had an irrepressible sense of humour and was not about to be cowed by the dour Dr Traherne. Instead of snapping back at him, she smiled and leant forward confidentially.

'I tell you what,' she said, her solemn expression belied by the twinkle in her green eyes. 'I'll let you worry about your project, and you let me worry about my photography!'

Keir Traherne was obviously having difficulty controlling his temper. 'When you've quite finished making smart comments, we may as well go.' He glanced around. 'Where's your luggage?'

'Ah . . . good question.' Poppy turned up her palms in a gesture of ignorance.

'Don't tell me you've lost your bags!'

'Well, it rather looks that way.' She knew her breezy attitude would annoy him, but so much the better.

Keir swore and raked his fingers through his dark hair. 'Here we go! I knew a female photographer would be nothing but trouble. Not only have I had to waste a whole day hanging round in this god-forsaken airport waiting for you to turn up, but now we've got to waste more time chasing up your luggage!'

'It's hardly my fault,' Poppy protested, stung out of her airiness. 'It's not as if I single-handedly sabotaged the plane or threw my bags out somewhere over the Sahara, just to cause you trouble.'

For a moment they glared at each other. In spite
of his shirt and tie, Keir looked cool and comfortable, Poppy noted resentfully. Her own white cut-
off jeans were sticking to her clammily, and her
shirt hung limp and crumpled.

Keir sighed. 'Look, I'm sorry. We've got
a . . . problem up in Adouaba and it's vital that I
see the government officials in Mbuka before it gets
out of hand. I spent all last week trying to fix up
a meeting and finally arranged it for today, but then
I heard from Thorpe Halliwell that they were
sending you out, so I had to cancel to come and
pick you up.' He looked at Poppy with renewed
exasperation. 'I was lucky to rearrange it for
tomorrow morning. If you'd been on time, we could
have driven up to Mbuka this afternoon, but it's
too dangerous to drive on these roads in the dark,
so we'll have to spend the night here now and leave
very early tomorrow . . . which means we'd better
report the loss of your luggage now.'

Poppy trotted after him as he strode off to a dark,
poky office. He might not be very pleased to see
her, but at least he wasn't going to abandon her
here. Keir dealt briskly with the formalities while
she stood feeling hot, tired and inadequate in the
face of his competence. Firing questions at her as
he filled in the sheaf of forms apparently required
to report the loss, he translated for a listless official
in rapid French.

'Don Jones told me Cameroon was English-
speaking,' Poppy said, as they handed back the
forms and made their way outside.

'Officially it's bilingual, and Adouaba is in an anglophone province, but even there you'll find that most officials speak French, so it helps if you speak some. Do you?'

'No.'

'Have you ever been on an expedition before?'

'No.'

'Do you know anything about the rain forest?'

'Er . . . no.'

'I can tell you're going to be a real asset to the project,' Keir commented acidly.

Poppy would have liked to have been able to boast about some other talent she possessed, but couldn't think of anything. 'I'm a very good photographer,' she offered.

Keir merely snorted, obviously unimpressed. He unlocked the door of a battered old Land Rover and held it open for her before going round to the driver's side and climbing in himself. 'Any idiot can hold a camera. I could have taken some photographs if that's all that Thorpe Halliwell wanted. Or was this trip a "jolly" dreamed up by Don Jones for his little girlfriend?'

'One, I'm not little; two, I'm not Don Jones's girlfriend as he is very happily married; and three, it certainly hasn't been very jolly so far,' Poppy pointed out crossly. 'And if you think you can take the same photographs as I can, all I can say is that you don't know very much about photography, so it's just as well Thorpe Halliwell did send a professional photographer. After all, they've given you a lot of sponsorship as well as some computer equipment. The least they deserve are some decent publicity photographs in return.'

'As you say, I suppose I'm lumbered with you, but there are a few things I'd like to make clear here and now. You may be Thorpe Halliwell's blue-eyed girl, but I'm the leader of this expedition and, out here, what I say goes. That means that you'll do as you're told. Is that clear?'

Biting back a flippant comment, Poppy shrugged in resignation. 'Where are we going now?'

'We'll have to spend tonight in a hotel. It's not far.'

Poppy sat wide-eyed as the Land Rover nosed its way through streets crowded with people and stalls. Music blared tinnily out of the darkness and the headlights of the cars threw faces into sharp relief. 'I may as well warn you now that we'll be sharing a room,' Keir said brusquely, as they drew up outside a shabby hotel. 'Hotels in Douala are extremely expensive, and we can't afford to pay for two rooms just because you've got maidenly scruples.'

'You didn't seem to think I'd have scruples about having an affair with a married man, so I'm hardly likely to worry about sharing a room with someone like you.' Poppy wasn't a prude, but the idea was strangely unsettling, and irritation with herself sharpened her voice.

He stopped in the middle of lifting her camera bag out of the Land Rover. 'What do you mean, someone like me?'

'Well, you haven't exactly bowled me over with your charm,' Poppy said bravely, 'or vice versa, so the fact that you're a man and I'm a woman doesn't bother me at all.' If she said it confidently enough she might even convince herself!

'Nothing seems to bother you,' Keir commented unfairly. 'Don't you take anything seriously?'

'When you're as accident-prone as I am, you can't afford to take things too seriously. And anyway, I can't see that I'd get much sympathy from you if I started making a fuss, would I?'

Unexpectedly, he grinned. 'How right you are!' The austere face broke into warmth and humour and Poppy's heart did a slow somersault, settling back into place with an alarming thump. She hadn't imagined that he could look like that.

'We'll have to leave early tomorrow morning, so I suggest we go and have a quick meal straight away, and then have an early night.'

Poppy longed to change her sticky clothes, but had to be content with washing her face and hands and examining her crumpled reflection glumly. She might not make a fuss, but it would have been nice to have had something clean and fresh to change into... At least the room had twin beds. For one awful moment she had thought she might even have to be casual about sharing a bed, and she didn't think she would have been up to that, no matter how nice Keir's smile was! Things would be difficult enough as they were, keeping up the pretence of unconcern when her heart thumped uncomfortably at the mere thought of such enforced intimacy with a man like Keir Traherne.

They ate in a small, dark restaurant near the hotel. 'There isn't any choice,' said Keir, after ordering rapidly in French, 'so you just have to have whatever is fresh.'

'What's on the menu tonight?'

'Porcupine.'

'Porcu——' Poppy broke off to peer at Keir. 'You're not serious?'

He looked down his nose at her. 'Why not? It's very good.'

A young boy put two glasses of beer on the table. Poppy eyed hers dubiously. She hated beer. 'Isn't there anything else?'

'No,' said Keir.

'Oh.' She sighed, and took a reluctant sip. 'Tell me a bit more about the expedition,' she invited, to take her mind off the taste. 'Don told me you had about thirty scientists working out here.'

He nodded. 'Some of the oldest primary rain forest in the world is here in Cameroon. The idea of the project was really to get a large team of scientists from different specialities and give them the administrative back-up to enable them to carry out research from the forest floor to the top of the canopy, so that we can get a clearer idea of how different ecosystems are related. The more we know about how the forest works, the better we can protect it.'

The candlelight lit up the angular planes of his face as he toyed with his fork, drawing patterns on the rather grubby tablecloth. 'So here we've got an opportunity for specialists to work out in the field and pick each other's brains for a few months without having to worry about all the bureaucracy and logistics that go into supplying them with fresh rations and ensuring that the paperwork's in order. We deal with all that in Adouaba.'

'It sounds great,' said Poppy, trying to remember just how his face had changed when he smiled. 'Are you doing research as well as all the administration?'

'Yes, but I've got two assistants doing most of the field-work. I'm mainly concerned with analysing the information gathered on the computer—courtesy of Thorpe Halliwell—and compiling a report which I hope will allow us to continue working out here.' A note of bitterness crept into his voice. 'A month ago I'd have thought it was a foregone conclusion that we'd get permission, but now I'm not so sure.'

'Why not?' Poppy suddenly found that she had been watching his mouth and hastily dragged her attention back to what he was saying.

'The usual reason—money.' In sudden disgust, Keir pushed the fork away from him and reached for his beer. 'Just when everything seems to be going well, some smart aleck from London turns up. He talks about development schemes, but what he's *thinking* about is cutting down the forest so that he can get at the minerals he imagines are in the ground. It's rubbish, of course—no one in their right minds would look for minerals there—but if he manages to persuade the government that he can produce lots of money out of thin air—thin earth is a better word!—we can wave goodbye to the project——'

He broke off and glanced over at Poppy, who was watching him, a little surprised by his vehemence. He was obviously passionately committed to his project and instinctively she warmed to him, revising her initial impression of a man too coldly efficient to care much about anything. She was very aware of his solid presence on the other side of the table. There was something about his compact strength that was both reassuring and unsettling. He was still neat and dark, but somehow he didn't seem so ordinary any more. Suddenly Poppy found herself wondering about what it would be like undressing in front of him, slipping into bed, knowing that he was so close...

An awkward silence was broken by the waiter placing a plate of an unappetising brown claggy lump in front of Poppy. She looked at it, then at Keir.

'Is this it?'

'That's it,' he said gravely, amusement lurking in his eyes as he watched her cut off a piece with some reluctance.

To Poppy's relief, it tasted a lot better than it looked, rather like gamey chicken. 'What's this?' She was inspecting a saucer of a thick rust-red sauce. Without waiting for Keir's reply, she put a dollop on a piece of meat and popped it in her mouth.

Keir winced and for a moment Poppy wondered what he was doing. The next instant she felt her eyes bulge and her tongue shrivel as the top of her head threatened to explode. The tears were streaming down her cheeks as she fumbled for her glass, unable to do more than croak 'Aaah...aaah.'

To her fury, Keir began to laugh. 'That's the local chilli sauce. It's rather hot.'

'Rather hot!' Poppy gasped. 'That's like saying winter in the Antarctic can be a bit cool.' She pushed the saucer away from her nervously. 'That stuff's not safe!' She took another long swallow of beer and shot Keir a resentful glance, horribly aware of her red face and streaming eyes.

'Serves you right for being so rash,' Keir said unsympathetically. He beckoned for some more beer and Poppy accepted another glass gratefully, forgetting her dislike in her desperation to cool her burning throat. 'It's a sound policy in places like this to take things slowly—you'll find that the locals do. When you're out in the jungle you can't just grab a fruit that looks good to eat; you have to try a little bit to see if it's poisonous or not.'

Poppy sighed. It wasn't in her nature to take things slowly and carefully. 'It all sounds very frustrating.'

'Better to be frustrated than dead,' Keir commented shortly. He looked across the table and met Poppy's bright innocent gaze. 'Thorpe Halliwell must be out of their minds sending someone like you here. How on earth did you get involved with them?'

'I met Don Jones when I was doing some freelance photography for one of their subsidiaries. He invited me to take a series of photos of their computers and logo in unusual situations—you know, in a Hebridean croft, on a boat, that kind of thing.'

She paused, remembering how she had first heard about Cameroon.

'How do you fancy a trip to West Africa?' Don
Jones had asked, tilting back his chair and watching
her with a speculative expression. Don was the
public relations director for Thorpe Halliwell and
not a man given to idle questions.

'Africa?' Poppy had queried, intrigued but
slightly apprehensive. She had never been anywhere like Africa before.

'More specifically, Cameroon. The chairman was
delighted with that last assignment. Thorpe
Halliwell's image has rocketed since the public have
started associating us with being used outside the
normal office context—and that's largely thanks to
your photos, Poppy. They seem to have caught the
public imagination. In fact, the whole campaign has
been so successful that we're going to pursue the
idea of linking Thorpe Halliwell with unusual situations. We've just agreed major sponsorship of a
scientific expedition in the West African rain forest.
The leader of the expedition is a very high-powered
scientist. I haven't met him, but he's got an impressive reputation—a world authority on the rain
forest, I believe. Ecology seems to be the buzz-word
at the moment, and we should be able to get a lot
of PR mileage out of it. It isn't an obvious as-
sociation between high technology and rain forest,
but it's that contrast we want to play on.'

'And you want me to go out and take some PR
shots?'

'That's right. A scientist working at a computer
in the middle of the jungle. The Thorpe Halliwell
logo right up in the rain forest canopy. That kind
of thing. We liked the way the eye was drawn to

the logo in that last set of photos you did. It was quite unobtrusive, but somehow you found yourself looking for it. We'd like the same effect this time. Well, how do you feel about it?'

Poppy had only recently gone freelance, and was not in a position to turn down assignments, particularly not from a company like Thorpe Halliwell. And anyway, she'd thought, she might never get another chance to visit Africa. Opportunities like this were not to be missed. Poppy had pushed aside lingering doubts. 'I'd love to go,' she'd said firmly.

'Great!' Don Jones had let his chair crash back to the floor. 'We'll fix up all the details with Dr Traherne. All you have to do is get on the plane.'

Well, it hadn't been quite that easy. Poppy remembered the frantic rush to get ready; leaving all her newly purchased film in a taxi, breaking the zip on her case, fainting when she had her vaccinations . . . as usual, she had lurched from disaster to disaster, and now here she was in darkest Africa eating porcupine with a misogynist!

'Still, it's unusual to find a young woman given this kind of assignment, surely?' Keir asked, when she had told him a little more about her work.

'It's more unusual to find someone with your views on women,' Poppy retorted. He seemed to have real hang-up about women. For the first time it occurred to her to wonder if he was married, but she dismissed the thought almost immediately. He had a very independent look about him. Had he had some bitter disappointment in love? Had his heart been broken when he was young, turning against women for ever? She eyed him speculatively, but was forced to acknowledge reluctantly that Keir did not look like a romantic type. He didn't even look like a man with a heart to be broken! No, Keir's reactions to women would be purely practical.

Obscurely piqued, she swept on, 'It's extraordinary how men like you cling to the stereotyped idea of women. I mean, you're a scientist; you must know about the theory of evolution.' Keir gave her a cold look, but she ignored him, determined to make her point. 'And evolution has now got to the point where most people recognise that a woman is just as intelligent and just as capable of doing a job as any man!'

She finished triumphantly, but Keir was unimpressed. 'That's the theory, of course, but in my experience there's a big difference between theory and practice. In any case, my objection to a woman was not so much as a photographer as a disruptive influence.'

'I've no intention of being disruptive, as you call it,' Poppy said grandly. 'I've been on assignments with men before and after a while they don't even notice that I'm a woman any more. I'm just . . . one of the lads.'

Keir lifted an eyebrow. 'They sound like very odd men.' His penetrating eyes travelled from her soft, generous mouth down to the shadowy hollow at her throat before dropping to the swell of her breasts beneath her shirt. To her horror, Poppy felt a tingling blush steal over her, and she ran her tongue in unconscious suggestion over lips that were suddenly dry.

'You don't look like one of the lads to me, Penelope,' he went on, his voice very deep and low.

Poppy swallowed. She had an odd feeling in the pit of the stomach which had nothing to do with the porcupine. Her eyes flickered over to Keir. He was watching her with light, unreadable eyes and she felt her heart begin to thump slowly, slowly against her ribs. What on earth was the matter with her? She drew an uneven breath, desperate to break the taut silence. 'Would you mind not calling me Penelope?' she asked, cringing at the nervous sound of her laugh. 'Everybody calls me Poppy. Penelope always makes me feel as if I'm in trouble.'

'Let's hope that we don't have much cause to call you Penelope, then.' Keir drained his glass and stood up, abruptly breaking the tension. His voice was dry, and Poppy wondered if he had even noticed. 'But on present form it seems rather doubtful.'

The damp heat seemed to envelop Poppy as they walked back to the hotel, clinging to the back of her neck, wrapping itself round her body and making even breathing an effort. Exhaustion had suddenly overwhelmed her and she was glad of Keir's silence.

The room hadn't seemed so small before. Now Keir seemed to fill it, and she moved around very

carefully, nervous in case she touched him acci-
dentally. In the bathroom, she rinsed out her
underwear and then realised that she had nothing
to sleep in. Eventually she wrapped a towel round
her and sidled back into the room, leaping into bed
as soon as Keir's back was turned and pulling the
sheet up to her chin. She had never felt so aware
of being naked before. She lay stiffly, facing the
wall, and if Keir noticed her tension he gave no sign
of it. He just carried on methodically preparing for
bed. Poppy could hear the sounds of him undressing, the creak of the bed opposite as he settled
himself in, the click of the light being switched off.
He grunted goodnight, and she murmured a reply,
unnerved by her sense of mingled relief and
anticlimax.

She felt ridiculous. What had she expected? That
he was going to throw himself down on her and
make wild, passionate love? It would hardly have
been Keir Traherne's style! He had made it very
plain that he had no time for women, and, even if
he had, he certainly wouldn't have wasted any on
an irritating scruff like Poppy Sharp.

With a tiny little sigh, Poppy rolled on to her
back. In spite of her tiredness, it was some time
before she slept. An air conditioner rattled noisily
in the darkness and she lay listening to it, resenting
Keir's ability to fall asleep so easily. Bright moonlight through the wooden shutters at the window
barred his sleeping form on the other bed.

Poppy turned on her side and watched the way
it illuminated the high cheekbones and the unex-

pectedly sensual mouth. It was not a mouth that belonged to a tidy man, she thought drowsily, and fell asleep at last wondering exactly what lay beneath Dr Traherne's efficient exterior.

CHAPTER TWO

'IT'S five o'clock.'

Poppy surfaced to the sound of Keir's voice, full of the smug satisfaction of those who had no trouble being wide awake at unearthly hours of the morning. She groaned and rolled over, pulling the sheet over her head. Poppy was not a morning person.

'Come on, Poppy, wake up.' Keir shook her shoulder and she opened one baleful eye.

'Leave me alone!'

'I'd be delighted to leave you behind, unless you hurry up,' he threatened. 'I want to be on the road by half-past five.'

Poppy struggled to sit upright, remembering just in time to take the sheet with her. Her eyes felt gummed together, and she rubbed them with her knuckles like a child. 'It's still dark,' she grumbled, then regretted it as Keir switched on the overhead light. Wincing at the glare from the naked bulb, she covered her eyes with her hand and peered at Keir resentfully through her fingers. 'I want to go back to sleep.'

'Well, you can't. Now come on, get up, or I'll put you under the cold shower myself!'

'You wouldn't dare——' Poppy began, but lost her nerve as Keir took a step towards her. She wouldn't put it past the man, she decided after another look at his face. 'All right, all right,' she grumbled, wrapping the sheet round her toga-fashion and hobbling to the bathroom. She blinked at her bleary-eyed reflection in the mildewed mirror. 'Bleuch!'

She looked an absolute mess. It was all too easy to imagine what Keir must have thought. Poppy had a vague memory of feeling disturbingly aware of him last night, but she shrugged it away. She must have been more tired than she realised. It wasn't as if he was the kind of man she normally found attractive. She had never liked dour, dis-approving men. No, Keir Traherne was most defi-nitely not her type.

The shower was little more than a trickle of cold water, but at least it helped wake her up. Poppy turned her face up to it and let it wash the sleep away before shampooing her hair vigorously.

'Hurry up!' Keir banged on the door. 'You only need a quick shower, for heaven's sake, not a com-plete beauty treatment.'

Poppy made a face at the door. 'Oh, shut up,' she muttered, but not loud enough for him to hear. His briskness was infuriating at this hour of the day.

'What?' he shouted over the noise of the shower. His hearing must have been as keen as his eyes.

Or else he just had big ears, Poppy thought sourly. 'I said, I'm coming,' she shouted back, but lingered perversely in the bathroom for as long as she could. Let him wait; it was the least he deserved for waking her up so early.

She could hear him pacing up and down, muttering to himself, as she tugged a comb through her curls, and she grinned at herself in the mirror. It felt good to be clean again, even at five in the morning. Slipping quickly into her bra and pants, which had dried overnight, and, shrugging herself into her blue shirt, she opened the door just as Keir raised his fist to hammer on it once more.

'Ready!' she said with a bright smile.

Keir lowered his arm with a suspicious look. 'About time,' he grunted. His eyes dropped to her bare legs and he turned away abruptly. 'What is it that women do in bathrooms that takes them five times as long as a man?'

'I had to wake myself up to start with,' Poppy pointed out. 'I'm a bit slow in the mornings.'

'I'd already gathered that,' Keir said caustically. 'Now look, will you please just hurry up? We should have been away from here a quarter of an hour ago.'

She paused in the act of stepping into her trousers. 'We're only fifteen minutes late? I thought from the way you were carrying on that we were at least three hours overdue.'

'We will be unless you get a move on,' Keir said in a cold voice.

Poppy finished buttoning her shirt with a studied lack of haste, wrinkling her nose at the stain where the man in the next seat on the plane had spilt coffee all over her. 'I wish I had some other clothes to put on,' she said, and rubbed at the stain ineffectually with her finger. 'This is filthy.'

'It really doesn't matter what you wear,' Keir said impatiently. 'You'll be even dirtier by the time we get to Adouaba anyway.'

'Why are you looking so smart, then?' Poppy threw an accusing look at Keir's crisp white shirt, tan trousers and tie. He had a good figure, she acknowledged to herself reluctantly, and he was obviously very fit; he might be dressed for an office, but he gave the impression of a man who could as easily jog up a mountain as sit at a desk.

'There's a tarmac road some of the way to Mbuka, so I should be able to stay fairly clean until then. It's essential to make the right impression whenever doing business here. You can't just turn up in shorts and a T-shirt and expect people to treat you with respect—which is why I won't be introducing you to anyone as part of the project today. You don't exactly give an impression of smart professionalism.'

'It would be easier if I had something clean to wear,' Poppy pointed out.

'We'll get you some more clothes when we get to Adouaba—*if* we get to Adouaba today.' Keir looked at his watch pointedly. 'Are you ready yet?'

'Almost.' Poppy finished throwing everything haphazardly into the old satchel she carried everywhere instead of a handbag, and stood up with a cheerful grin. 'All present and correct! What's for breakfast?'

'Nothing,' Keir said shortly, picking up his bag. 'We're late enough as it is. You can have something to eat in Mbuka. Now, come on!'

It was still dark as the Land Rover pulled out of the hotel car park, and by the time the sky began to lighten they were bowling along an empty road lined by endless rows of palm trees and she began to sit up and take notice. Keir drove fast, apparently unconcerned by the need to veer round pot-holes and avoid the goats and dogs which wandered on to the road with sublime indifference to the roar of approaching vehicles. Poppy flinched as a swerve round a particularly wide hole threatened to take them into the path of an oncoming truck.

'Do you have to go quite so fast?' she said, uncovering her eyes.

'I want to get to Mbuka in good time.' Keir threw her a disgusted glance. 'It's been quite good going so far, but the tarmac road is going to end soon and that'll slow us down.'

Sure enough, barely a minute later the tarmac ended abruptly and they bumped down on to a dirt road. Immediately a cloud of dust rose up behind them. The Land Rover jolted and juddered over the ruts and Poppy clung to her seat nervously. In the bright morning light it seemed an incredibly dilapidated vehicle. The dashboard was bare metal and a confusion of wires hung beneath it. The seats were no more than strips of canvas hung on a metal frame.

'Are you sure this vehicle is safe?' Poppy asked, looking dubiously at a hole in the floor.

'Safe? Of course it's safe!'

'That's what they said about the Titanic, and that was in a lot better shape than this.'

'Look, there's nothing wrong with it. This may not be the most luxurious model, but it's perfectly adequate,' Keir said defensively. 'Tarmac roads are in short supply round here. You need a vehicle that doesn't grind to a halt at the first patch of mud. I've covered quite a bit of Africa in this old girl, and she's never let me down yet.' He gave the steering wheel an affectionate pat.

Poppy looked unconvinced. 'You're obviously one of those men who prefers cars to women,' she said with a naughty look.

'They're certainly a lot less trouble,' Keir said nastily. 'As long as you know how to handle it properly, a car will always do exactly what you want it to do.'

'You could say the same thing about women,' Poppy pointed out.

Keir's mouth twitched. 'Not in my experience.' What *was* his experience? she wondered. She didn't really know anything about him. He might be married for all she knew, or perhaps there was a faithful girlfriend waiting patiently at home, not getting in the way? Poppy pushed aside a ridiculous feeling of bleakness at the thought and concentrated on what Keir was saying. 'At least vehicles don't insist on having the last word.'

'It doesn't sound like any car I've ever had.' Poppy pulled herself together, remembering morosely a series of disastrous vehicles. 'Mine always manage to get the better of me—not to mention my bank account.'

'If you run your cars in the same way you seem to run the rest of your life, I'm not surprised,' said Keir. 'You seem to be a walking disaster area.'

Poppy opened her mouth to protest, but wasn't quite able to deny it. 'My brothers used to call me the Jinx,' she confessed with a sigh. 'But it isn't me. Things just . . . happen to me.'

'Accidents don't *just happen*,' Keir said unsympathetically. 'That's just an illogical mind making excuses for lapses of concentration.'

'And *that* is the kind of super-scientific attitude that takes no account at all of the mysteries of life! Why is it that a machine breaks down as soon as I so much as look at it?'

'Operator error,' Keir said in a perfunctory voice. 'Machines only break down if you're not using them properly. It's only a matter of reading the instructions.'

Poppy rolled her eyes. 'Trust you to be the sort of man who reads the instructions! I'll bet you have all your books arranged in alphabetical order too!'

'It seems a logical way to arrange them,' Keir said stiffly, after a tiny pause. 'It's all a question of organisation, and I'd appreciate it if you could organise yourself enough to stay out of trouble while you're out here. I've got enough problems on my plate without having to worry about you.'

Poppy decided against arguing. 'If this meeting goes well, that'll solve most of your problems, won't it?'

'It would be nice to think so, but unlikely!' Keir looked grim. 'The development company aren't likely to give up without a fight, and they've plenty of money and smooth talking at their disposal. And we not only want to secure what we've got, we want to extend the project. The scientists want to do some research further into the forest before the rains come, and we can't do anything without permits and letters and stamps and authorisations and lord knows what else from everyone with any conceivable connection with our work. Nothing's easy in Cameroon! But nothing's going to get done until they've made a decision about this development offer. That's why it's so vital that I get to this meeting and convince the government that it's not worth risking all we've achieved for some nonsensical idea about everyone getting rich quick.'

'What time is the meeting?' asked Poppy.

'Eight-thirty. It was the only time I could pin him down for. If your plane had been on time, we could have driven to Mbuka yesterday.'

'Is it much further?'

'About another hour.'

Poppy glanced at her watch and added ten minutes to allow for the fact that it ran continuously slow. 'We'll be in plenty of time,' she said comfortably.

Thirty seconds later, the Land Rover began pulling to one side. Keir swore with vivid fluency as he braked, and jumped out. Poppy followed more cautiously. This part of the road was shaded from the sun by heavy growth on each side, and the vehicle had stopped at an angle in a patch of slippery mud. One of the back tyres was ominously flat. Keir kicked it in disgust.

'You obviously weren't concentrating,' Poppy murmured, all innocence.

'What's that?' Keir looked up from his examination of the tyre.

'You've got a puncture,' she said, deciding not to push her luck.

His eyes were cold and grey. 'Really?' he said, with heavy sarcasm. 'What a good thing you're here, otherwise I'd never have guessed.'

'There's no need to be unpleasant,' Poppy said loftily. 'I was only trying to help.'

'Stating the obvious isn't much help.' He straightened. 'You'll have to change the wheel.'

'Me? Why me?'

'Because, as I've already explained, I need to look relatively smart to see the SDO, and I won't be if I have to change the wheel. It won't make any difference if you look a mess.'

'Thanks!'

'For heaven's sake, is this any time to worry about what you look like?' Keir had opened the back of the Land Rover and was pulling out some tools.

'You are,' Poppy pointed out.

With an effort, Keir brought his temper under control. 'Poppy, could you just stop arguing and change the bloody wheel?'

'Please?' she suggested sweetly.

'Could you please change the wheel?' Keir amended through clenched teeth.

'Certainly!' Poppy gave him her best smile and picked up the jack from the grass. She turned the pieces uncertainly in her hands. 'Er...how does this work?'

'Don't tell me you've never used a jack before!'

'Of course I have...just not like this.'

'And then they wonder why I don't want women on the project!' Keir rubbed his forehead in frustration. 'Use your eyes, woman. What shape is this? And this? Don't you think they might fit together? Now *that* goes there. I'd have thought a child of five could have worked that out.'

'Not unless it had read the instructions first,' Poppy said sullenly as she crouched down to place the jack under the vehicle and began pumping up the Land Rover. It was already hot and sticky and the mud squelched beneath her feet.

'Loosen the nuts first,' Keir ordered, and tossed her the wrench, which promptly dropped out of Poppy's fumbling grasp into the mud. She picked it up with distaste, holding it gingerly between finger and thumb.

'Ugh! It's all slimy. What did you throw it like that for?'

'I was stupid enough to think you might have sufficient co-ordination to catch it. Why don't you stop complaining and get on with it? I seem to remember that last night you were full of how you could do just as good a job as a man. Now's your chance to prove it.'

'I said I was just as good a photographer as any man. I didn't say I wanted to be a mechanic!' Still grumbling, Poppy gritted her teeth and stamped on the wrench handle to release the nut. 'This is ruining my fingernails!'

She struggled with the awkward task while Keir stood looking impatient and glancing at his watch. At last it was done. By the time she had finished, Poppy was covered in mud. She had slipped twice lifting off the flat wheel and was sorely tempted to throw it at Keir when he laughed.

'I'm sorry,' he had the grace to apologise when she glared at him. 'I was just wondering how it was possible for anyone—even you!—to get quite so dirty in such a short time.'

Poppy wiped the sweat off her upper lip with her arm, leaving yet another muddy smear, and smiled reluctantly. 'I hope this meeting is worth it!' Wearily she threw the tools into the back of the Land Rover. 'That's it, I think.'

'Good girl.' Keir smiled at her, and Poppy felt something tighten in her chest. It was the first time he had actually smiled with approval at her and she felt absurdly pleased at his laconic praise. For a while she forgot about the mud that caked her and the rumbling hunger in her stomach, thinking about the way the smile creased his cheeks and lit an unexpected warmth in the cool eyes.

She studied him covertly beneath her lashes as they drove on at a punishing pace to make up for lost time. He *wasn't* handsome...no, definitely not handsome...and yet there was an indefinable quality about him that made one look twice. Strong eyebrows and nose gave him his formidable look, she decided, and although his chin was equally uncompromising that mouth definitely suggested a man not quite as coldly logical as he appeared. Poppy remembered that she had lain awake studying his mouth, and dragged her eyes away as a disquieting warmth uncurled without warning deep inside.

Her gaze dropped to his hands. Strong and sure, they rested confidently on the steering-wheel. With more than a touch of envy, she wondered what it was like to be someone so quietly competent, so obviously in control of the situation, so unlike herself. Unconsciously, she sighed, and forced herself to look out of the window instead.

They reached Mbuka after a bone-shattering ride, with two minutes to spare before Keir's meeting was due to begin. The Land Rover pulled up outside the grandly named Boulangerie Moderne and Keir handed her some money.

'You can sit in there and have a coffee or something. The doughnuts are good. I'm not sure how long I'll be, so can you please just stay there? Don't wander off or talk to anyone or...do anything! Just stay there until I come.'

'Am I allowed to breathe?' Poppy asked with an innocent face, but Keir was unamused.

'Only if you can do it without getting into trouble—which I doubt!'

Poppy watched the dust settle in his wake before turning and walking stiffly into the Boulangerie. Inside, it was dark and rather dingy. She had a Coke and a deliciously warm doughnut and began to feel better. Deciding that she had earned it, she bought another doughnut, and sat looking out on to the street which was a chaotic confusion of people, yellow taxis, carts and goats. The dust hung heavily in the air.

'Rather disorganised, isn't it?' An unmistakably English voice broke into her thoughts, and she looked up quickly in surprise. The man standing by her table looked as English as his voice, with blond hair falling over his forehead and warm blue eyes. Without thinking, she smiled back, and, taking her smile as invitation, he sat down opposite her.

'I hope I'm not being too forward, but there aren't many expatriates round here, so I know you must be new here.'

Poppy, irrepressibly friendly herself, found it impossible to resist his almost tangible charm. It was certainly a welcome change from Keir's dourness! 'Very new,' she said. 'I only arrived last night.'

'In that case, welcome to Cameroon! I'm Ryan Saunders.' Poppy beamed over at her companion as they shook hands. 'You don't appear to have a rucksack, so you can't be a traveller,' he went on.

'Not exactly. I'm on my way to Adouaba to join a scientific expedition.' She nodded her head at her camera bag. 'I'm a photographer.'

'Well, well.' Ryan leaned back in his chair and eyed her appraisingly. 'You must be with Keir Traherne, then. Quite a formidable character, isn't he?'

There was an odd note in his voice that made Poppy pause. 'You know Keir?'

'It's not all that surprising,' Ryan said easily. 'It's a small community of Brits, as I said. In fact, I've just seen him on his way to the senior district officer. He looked as if he was in a tearing hurry, didn't even have time to say hello.'

'Well, he was a bit late for a meeting, I think,' Poppy explained. For some reason she found it hard to imagine Keir passing the time of day with the carelessly charming Ryan Saunders. 'I'm waiting for him to finish, and then we're going on up to Adouaba.'

'I'm afraid you're in for a long wait—I've been at the SDO's myself this morning, and things are happening even slower than usual.' Ryan glanced at his watch. 'It's a pity I've got to get going, otherwise I could have shown you round a bit.'

Poppy stifled a pang of disappointment. Quite apart from the fact that Ryan Saunders was an undeniably attractive man, she was enjoying having some uncritical company for a change!

'I really am sorry I have to go,' Ryan was saying, holding her hand a little longer than was necessary, 'but I hope we'll meet again in Adouaba—in fact, I'll make sure we do!'

It was hard to imagine anyone more different from Keir, Poppy reflected watching Ryan Saunders stroll off with his hands in his pockets. Keir would shudder at the thought of holding her hand and as for laying on the charm... Unable to visualise the scene, Poppy turned back to gaze out of the window with a tiny, almost wistful sigh.

This was really her first sight of Africa. Poppy finished her doughnut and licked her fingers thoughtfully. If Keir was going to be as long at his oh, so important meeting as Ryan had implied, it seemed stupid not to explore a little. Surely she could spend half an hour looking round and be back here without his even knowing she had gone?

'Just stay there.' Keir's voice echoed in her ears, but Poppy pushed the memory firmly aside as she stepped out into the bright sunlight. A small boy balancing an enormous tray of sugarcane on his head walked past her and she followed him across the road to the market.

Imposing-looking women with skins as black and shiny as aubergines and wide, white smiles presided over piles of tomatoes, yams and pineapples, or metal bowls heaped high with grain. The women wore flamboyantly patterned materials and matching head-dresses and they called out to Poppy as she passed. 'You need onions?' 'Eh! I have good pineapple!'

Poppy smiled and shook her head. Her fingers itched to take out her camera. Eventually she stopped at a stall and bought some bananas. They were laid out with unconscious artistry on a rickety wooden table with piles of papaya and avocados.

'Could I take a picture?' Poppy held up her camera and met with a beaming smile. Tagged by curious children, she was soon clicking away happily.

Poppy had never been anywhere so colourful and intriguing. She had completely forgotten the time, forgotten what an odd sight she must look covered in dried mud as she picked her way through goats and dogs and children slipping through the crowd with huge trays on their heads.

She was just thinking how different it all was from England when she walked past a British postbox. She stopped, looked back at it. Surely it couldn't be? But there it stood, bright red and uncannily familiar. Poppy traced the E.R. and crest thoughtfully with her finger. It was an odd reminder of colonialism, somehow more evocative than grand buildings or monuments. The contrast of the red pillar-box and the dusty African scene behind would make a wonderful photograph, she realised, unslinging her camera.

She was so absorbed in focusing and setting up the shot that she didn't hear the shouts behind her, and had only taken a couple of pictures when a hand fell on her shoulder. She turned to see a young gendarme, gesticulating angrily, and her eyes widened when she saw he had a gun.

'Is—er—something the matter?' she ventured.

It seemed that something was. The gendarme pointed at the camera and shouted at her in French, obviously frustrated by her failure to understand. Poppy shrugged helplessly, but kept a firm hold on her camera.

When it was clear that they weren't getting anywhere, the gendarme jerked his gun crossly and indicated that Poppy should go with him. Poppy sighed, but went. She was not about to start arguing with a gun, and, anyway, someone at the police station was bound to speak English.

An hour later she was still sitting there, trying to dredge up memories of her O level French. It was a depressing place. A gendarme was typing laboriously on an ancient manual typewriter, while another tipped back in his chair and smoked a cigarette with his jacket unbuttoned. An older man scratched his head in frustration. Judging by his impressive display of decorations, this was the officer in charge.

'Je suis avec Dr Keir Traherne,' Poppy tried at last in an excruciating accent.

The officer looked up, his eyes suddenly alert. 'Dr Traherne?'

She beamed with relief. *'Oui.'* Perhaps her French wasn't as bad as all that.

'Vous êtes sa femme?' He sounded surprised.

Unfortunately, the rapid question was beyond Poppy. *'Oui,'* she said firmly, wondering what he had asked.

Keir's name evidently meant something, for the officer suddenly gave her a charming smile and shouted at the smoker, who got up reluctantly and went out.

Silence fell. Poppy studied the portrait of the president which hung on the wall, and tried not to think about what Keir would say when he found her. *If* he found her. For the first time it occurred to Poppy to feel a little worried. She had a blithe optimism that carried her through most crises, but even so she felt a little out of her depth here. She had never actually been arrested before. Visions of being thrown into a dark cell never to be heard of again began to circle in her brain, and she shifted uncomfortably. Now the hollow clack of the typewriter seemed ominous, and the officer's rather bored expression menacing. Poppy linked her fingers in her lap and vowed never to argue with Keir again if only he would come and find her.

CHAPTER THREE

IT FELT like a lifetime, but was probably nearer twenty minutes later when she heard a quick step in the hall. Poppy looked up hopefully. When Keir appeared in the doorway, she let out her breath slowly, and gave him a dazzling smile of relief.

Her smile was not returned. Keir favoured her with a comprehensive look that successfully reduced her to two inches tall, and turned immediately to the officer.

They shook hands and exchanged pleasantries in rapid French. Judging by the hearty laughter, they knew each other well, Poppy thought, eyeing Keir surreptitiously from beneath her lashes. Funny how that laugh transformed him into a disquietingly attractive man. Perhaps it was fortunate that he didn't smile at her more often. Despite that look he had given her, the sight of his lean figure was inexpressibly comforting. He lacked Ryan Saunders's easy charm and boyish good looks, but still he looked overwhelmingly competent, and she relaxed back into her chair, confident in the knowledge that he would sort everything out.

Suddenly she became aware that she was being regarded by two pairs of unsympathetic eyes. Next to the soft brown of the officer's, Keir's eyes were flint-hard and his expression left Poppy in no doubt of his opinion of her. The camera lay accusingly on the desk.

'I gather you've been taking photographs in a prohibited place,' Keir said in a glacial voice. 'You'd better tell me exactly what you've been doing.'

'But I haven't been doing anything,' Poppy protested. 'I was taking a photo of a perfectly innocent postbox when I got a gun stuck in my ribs!'

Keir turned back to the officer and translated. After some discussion, he said to Poppy, 'Apparently the postbox is opposite an army barracks, and they therefore thought you might be taking photographs of military installations. However, I've explained that you are a very silly young woman, and that you weren't aware of the restrictions, and Henri here is prepared to let you go.'

Poppy opened her mouth, but he interrupted her before she could speak. 'Don't even think about arguing in here ... *Penelope*. Just get up, say "thank you" nicely and we'll go... although I'm sorely tempted to leave you here!'

She glared at him mutinously, forgetting her vow never to argue with him again. Green eyes met implacable grey. Biting her lip, Poppy got to her feet and retrieved her camera. 'Thank you—er—*merci*,' she said awkwardly.

Henri grinned and wrung her hand. Turning to Keir in high good humour, he said something in French which left him looking first surprised, and then appalled.

Poppy looked on, puzzled, as Keir shook his head vehemently, but he didn't enlighten her. Instead he took her elbow none too gently and they walked in taut silence to the Land Rover.

'Get in,' he said grimly, holding open the door. Poppy got in. The door was slammed shut after her, and then Keir got in beside her. He shoved the vehicle into gear and drove away from the police station with controlled fury.

'Can't I trust you alone for five minutes? I *told* you to stay at the Boulangerie. Was that so hard to understand?'

'I only wanted to look at the market.'

'But you didn't only look at the market, did you? You went and got yourself arrested. Only you could manage that!'

'How was I to know I wasn't allowed to take photographs?' Poppy said sulkily.

'All these countries are sensitive about foreigners taking photographs. I'd have thought your common sense would have told you to be careful about photographing near soldiers.'

'But I didn't even see the soldier! I was taking the postbox.'

Keir snorted. 'Only you would waste time taking a photo of a postbox you could see any day of the week at home. What in heaven's name did you want a picture of that for? It's cost me two hours of wasted time and several favours at the *gendarmerie*.'

'It was a wonderful picture,' said Poppy in a small voice.

'I don't care!' Keir almost shouted. 'You had no business to wander off when I had specifically asked you to stay in one place. Look at you!' His eyes swept over her disparagingly. 'What a bloody mess!

Do you realise how much damage you've done to the project's reputation today? We've spent a year building up trust here by making the right impression. And now that it matters more than ever you've destroyed it in five minutes. Henri's probably gone off to tell everyone that we've got the mud-women of Borneo working for us as spies!'

'I got muddy changing the rotten wheel for you, if you remember,' Poppy snapped back. 'Had I known I was going to be dragged off at gunpoint, then of course I'd have worn my ballgown!'

'I *knew* you were going to be trouble,' Keir went on, ignoring her. 'You've been in the country less than twenty-four hours, and already it's been nothing but a catalogue of disasters!'

'I don't see why you're making such a fuss. If it's such a sensitive issue taking photographs, why didn't you warn me?'

'I shouldn't have to warn you to use your common bloody sense! This is precisely why I wanted a photographer with some experience of Africa. I haven't time to act as nursemaid to a half-wit. But no, we had to have Miss Sharp and no one else! You must be the most inappropriately named person I've ever come across. Sharp suggests someone with at least a modicum of intelligence.'

'I would never have come if I'd known it was going to be like this.' Poppy's green eyes flashed dangerously. 'I'm here to take photographs, not take part in some survival course. I've hardly had any sleep, I've been jolted over a poor excuse for a road, I haven't had anything to eat except for a doughnut—well, two doughnuts—and I'm fed up with being lectured by a cross between Dr Livingstone and Hitler! You may think I'm a problem, but has it occurred to you that you're not exactly the best thing that's ever happened to me either?'

Keir's hands gripped the steering-wheel convulsively. 'I'm a very peaceful man normally, but if anyone could drive me to violence it would be you! And another thing! How dare you tell Henri you were my wife? The blood runs cold at the mere thought of being married to you!'

'I didn't!' Poppy's jaw dropped. This was evidently what Keir had been denying so forcibly as they left.

'Henri says you did. He had the nerve to congratulate me on my charming bride! It was bad enough your being associated with the project without it being thought that *I* was fool enough to actually marry someone like you!'

'He must have misunderstood something I said.' With some misgiving, Poppy remembered her confident reply to the question she had not understood, but she had no intention of telling Keir about that. 'Anyway,' she swept on, 'I can assure you the feeling is quite mutual. Personally, I can't think of a worse fate than being married to a fussy, bossy, clock-watching *tyrant* who arranges his books in alphabetical order!'

Still seething, she turned away to stare unseeingly out of the window. Horrible, horrible, hateful, hateful man! She wished she'd never come to Africa, never heard of Dr Traherne and the wretched rain forest. Why couldn't Thorpe

Halliwell have sponsored some worthy project in
Skegness instead?

They drove in stony silence along a road which
got progressively rougher and more rutted.
Whenever the Land Rover hit a deep rut, Poppy
would be thrown around in her seat with bone-
jarring impact, and any passing vehicle left her
coughing and spluttering in a cloud of choking red
dust.

By the time they reached Adouaba, Poppy was
bruised, battered and exhausted and wanted nothing
more than to lie down somewhere dark and quiet.
Adouaba itself was the end of the road. A strag-
gling town surrounded by forest, its chief occu-
pants seemed to be goats and chickens as far as
Poppy could make out as they drove through and
out along a narrow track with vegetation pressing
thickly on either side. They passed a few houses,
but at long last the Land Rover jerked to a halt
outside a low wooden building set back in a
clearing. A long veranda at the front was covered
with a luxuriant purple bougainvillaea, and the
garden was a tangle of exotic plants.

Keir jumped out and headed for the house, but
turned round when he realised that Poppy wasn't
behind him. She was still sitting in the cab, staring
blankly at the ground. Exhaustion had over-
whelmed her so suddenly that she felt physically
incapable of moving. Keir hesitated.

'Well, come on, then!'

Poppy just looked at him numbly. The next instant the door was opened and she was lifted bodily
out of the vehicle. Keir's face was close to hers, and

although he wore an expression of intense irritation she thought she could read concern in his eyes. Her own were dim with tiredness, and the usual sparkle in their green depths was missing. For a moment she felt his arms tighten about her, but so briefly that afterwards she wondered if she had imagined it.

In spite of her exhaustion, Poppy was over-whelmingly aware of the strength of his arms and the comforting solidity of his chest. The dislike that had buoyed her up during the long journey wavered in face of a confusing new emotion and she hardly knew whether to be glad or sorry when he set her on her feet on the veranda.

'All right?' he asked gruffly.

She nodded, suddenly unable to speak.

'Not like you to be lost for an answer,' Keir said, with a return to his caustic form, but it had the effect of making Poppy pull herself together.

She followed him into a large, sparsely furnished room, dim and cool. There were a few bamboo chairs, a desk covered in papers arranged in typically neat piles, and shelves stacked with books covering two walls. An uncluttered room for an un-cluttered man. Two ceiling fans slapped the heavy air lazily, and Poppy stood gratefully in the draught. She couldn't help comparing the room with her own flat, which obstinately resisted all attempts to impose order.

'This is Gabriel,' Keir introduced the shy house-boy. 'If you give him your clothes, he'll wash them for you. I'll give you a shirt or something to wear in the meantime.'

'Thank you,' said Poppy meekly, giving Gabriel a friendly smile.

'And this is your room.' Keir showed her into a large, high-ceilinged room, empty except for an iron bed and a wardrobe with doors which were tied together with string. Poppy eyed the bed longingly.

'The bathroom's next door if you'd like a shower,' Keir said with somewhat stilted politeness.

'I'd like to lie down for a few minutes first, if that's all right,' said Poppy with equal politeness, anxious not to break their unspoken truce. The effect was rather spoilt by a huge yawn.

'Don't sleep for too long. I want you to meet the rest of the project team tonight. We're invited out to supper.'

Poppy sat down stiffly on the bed. 'That's OK. I'll just put my feet up for a little while. I won't go to sleep.'

A warm finger was stroking the soft skin of her inner arm gently but insistently.

'Poppy?'

Poppy opened her eyes languidly to see Keir bending over her. For a long moment she stared into the cool grey eyes, wondering vaguely where she was but not really caring while those eyes were watching her. They held an unreadable expression as she smiled up sleepily, and then her mind was clearing and she sat up slowly, blinking herself awake.

'What time is it?'

'Seven o'clock. I thought you'd want a shower before we go out.'

'Seven o'clock.' She winced at the stiffness as she swung her legs hurriedly to the floor. 'I must have fallen asleep after all.'

'Obviously.' Keir's voice was dry, and Poppy suddenly became aware that she was wearing nothing but bra and pants. Not that Dr Traherne seemed to even notice, she reflected with a touch of an irritation that she did not pause to examine.

'I've left a clean shirt for you in the bathroom,' was all he said.

His lack of reaction to her feminine charms was understandable, Poppy thought despondently when she examined her mud-spattered reflection in the mirror. Her curls were caked with dust and she felt sticky all over.

The shower was bliss. Soaping herself vigorously, Poppy began to sing tunelessly, her natural optimism reasserting itself. She felt a million times better already, she decided, rubbing shampoo into an exuberant lather. True, it had been a hellish journey, but she was here now, and clean. She would take some marvellous photographs and make a real effort not to argue with Keir Traherne. Things could only get better.

Shampoo ran down her face and she screwed up her eyes as she reached down to grope blindly for the soap which had dropped at her feet. Her eyes were stinging and she lifted one hand to rub them just as the other closed over something live that scrabbled sickeningly beneath her fingers.

Poppy shrieked and jerked her hand away. Frantically blinking away shampoo, she shrank back and squinted down at her feet. An enormous cockroach squatted between her and the shower curtain, its antennae waving evilly. Poppy shuddered. Ugh! What a loathsome creature! She could swear it was leering at her.

'Poppy?' Keir knocked at the door impatiently. 'Are you all right in there?'

Poppy bit her lip. She could imagine only too well what kind of sarcastic comments she would receive if she told him she was pinned to the wall by a cockroach! Very cautiously, she began to edge round it, and put out a hand to steady herself on the shower curtain.

'I'm fi——' she managed, stepping out on to the tiled floor just as another cockroach dropped on to her, dislodged from its hiding place in the curtain. Instinctively she let out another yell and made a grab for the curtain as she felt herself overbalancing in her fright. Her weight proved too much for the shower rail, which crashed on to the tiles.

'What on earth's going on?' Keir had burst through the door and was staring at Poppy, who had somehow managed to stay upright and was regarding the mess with dismay. Her head was covered in a foamy crown of shampoo but she was otherwise stark naked.

This time Keir did notice. Expressionless, his eyes travelled slowly over her body, pink and glowing from the shower. Poppy's long-legged slimness was obvious, but the loose shirt she had worn had effectively disguised the full breasts and the honeyed perfection of her skin. Poppy was accustomed to think of herself as the gawky teenager she had been, oblivious to the way the long lines of her body had filled out imperceptibly to wanton beauty.

For a long moment she could only stand, held by cool, appraising eyes and unnerved by a rush of awareness that caught at her breath and left her tingling and confused. She felt her whole body flush with more than just embarrassment, and pulled herself together with an effort. Casting a harried glance around her, she snatched a towel off the rail and wrapped it round her.

'Nothing's going on,' she snapped, furious with herself and her own treacherous reactions as much as with Keir. How could she have just stood there like that? And how dared he watch her with those unsettling eyes of his?

'Nothing?' Keir cleared his throat and resumed his habitual exasperated expression. 'First there was a dreadful caterwauling, then squealing like a stuck pig...and I see you've managed to reduce my bathroom to a shambles somewhere along the line.'

'I was not squealing,' Poppy said coldly, ignoring his reference to her singing. 'I just...got a bit of a fright, that's all.' She met Keir's eyes defensively. 'The whole place is swarming with beastly creatures.'

'Were they responsible for pulling down the shower curtain?' he asked with an air of spurious interest.

'Well, no, not exactly. I was trying to escape when one ambushed me and I lost my balance.'

Keir looked at her. 'I had no idea my bathroom was such an exciting place.' He walked over to the shower and picked up the rail, propping it against the wall. Then he looked in the shower. 'Are these two the—er—swarm?'

Poppy hunched her shoulders sulkily and folded her arms. 'They felt like a swarm.'

To her fury, Keir began to laugh, a deep, attractive, masculine laugh that echoed round the tiled bathroom. He took off his shoe and disposed of the offending cockroaches unceremoniously, still laughing.

'I'm glad you find it so amusing.' Poppy was still in a huff as he tossed the corpses out of the window. 'Perhaps I could finish my shower now?' She tried to sound coldly dignified, but it was difficult with shampoo dripping down her nose.

Keir was waiting for her on the veranda. He was leaning on the rail with a beer in his hand and a brooding expression on his face as he stared out into the darkness.

Unobserved, Poppy watched him from the doorway. Even when relaxed and alone, he exuded an air of tough competence. She smiled to remember how she had expected Dr Traherne to be an absent-minded boffin pottering around the jungle. Nothing could be further from the truth! She found it impossible to imagine Keir Traherne pottering anywhere; a decisive stride was much more his style. And as for absent-minded, well, one glance into those penetrating grey eyes was enough to dispel *that* idea!

Keir turned as she moved forward into the dim light, still smiling at the thought. Her nut-brown hair was already drying in feathery curls about her

heart-shaped face and her smile deepened the
dimple lurking in her cheek. Keir's pale mint-
coloured shirt was cool and comfortable, but the
khaki shorts he had given her were so big that she
had had to tie them with string at the waist to keep
them up.

Slowly Keir's gaze moved upwards from her slim
legs to the swell of her breasts under the shirt and
the long neck emerging from the shadowy collar.
It was as if she were naked again. A tide of heat
washed over her as she remembered the way that
same gaze had lingered on her bare skin and she
found that she was holding her breath. His eyes
continued upwards until they met hers; for a long
moment they stared at each other in silence. Poppy
felt her heart begin to thud, slowly and
uncomfortably.

She smoothed the fine cotton of the shirt nervously as her eyes slid away from his. 'Thank you
for these.' She found it peculiarly disturbing to wear
his clothes. There was something almost intimate
about the touch of the cotton against her skin and
the shirt had a cool, clean, indefinably male smell
to it.

He brought her a glass and they leant together
on the railing. Poppy was excruciatingly aware of
him next to her as she searched desperately for
something to say to break the taut silence. The night
air was soft and dark, and vibrant with whirrs and
clicks and squeaks.'

'Are those crickets making that noise? I'd no idea
they could be so loud.'

'Among others. Wait until you get out into the forest. Sometimes you have to shout to make yourself heard over the insects.' His cool, intelligent face was alight with enthusiasm as he talked on. Poppy watched him and wondered what it would be like to reach out and touch his cheek with her fingers.

Appalled at the way her thoughts were leading her, she pulled herself up short. Something of her horror must have shown in her face because Keir broke off. 'Is something the matter?'

'No,' she said quickly. 'Er—who will be there tonight? I think Don Jones told me you had a deputy. Is he based here as well?'

'Guy Williams.' Keir nodded. 'And there's an administrative assistant as well.'

'What's his name?'

'Astrid Lewis.'

'*Astrid?*' Poppy put down her glass carefully. 'You mean you've got a woman on your team?'

'What of it?'

'Judging by the way you were carrying on in Douala, I gathered that women were the greatest threat to the rain forest since deforestation.'

'Don't be ridiculous,' Keir said irritably. 'It's true that I don't approve of women on the project for practical reasons, but Astrid is rather different.'

'You mean she's a man after all?'

Keir ignored her interruption. 'Astrid is an extremely efficient administrator. She's had a good deal of experience of this kind of work and she really knows what she's doing. I couldn't teach her anything about working in this kind of environment.'

'Quite a paragon, in fact.' Poppy was unprepared for the pinch of jealousy. She ought to have
been delighted to have found another woman for
support.

'She's a great asset,' Keir said reprovingly. 'I'm
first and foremost a scientist, and although I'm
dealing with the logistics of running the project we
need someone like Astrid who can deal with the
paperwork side of things.'

'I'm just surprised you appointed a woman, given
your views on the subject—or was she foisted on
you by a sponsor as well?'

'You don't have any experience of this kind of
life. Astrid has.'

'You mean that Astrid wouldn't turn a hair if she
was attacked by a cockroach?'

Keir's teeth gleamed briefly. 'She certainly
wouldn't have mistaken it for a swarm.'

'Bully for her!' Poppy stared crossly out into the
darkness and refused to ask herself why she dis-
liked the idea of the unknown Astrid so much.

Crickets whirred frenetically and the fragrance
of exotic plants drifted through the darkness as they
walked in edgy silence along the track. Once Poppy
stumbled into a rut, and Keir grasped her elbow to
steady her, but he dropped his hand almost immediately. Absently, she rubbed her arm where it
tingled still with the imprint of his fingers.

Astrid's house was a much smaller version of
Keir's and doubled as the project office. The walls
were covered with businesslike maps and charts and
a table in the corner bristled with radio equipment.
Astrid came out on to the veranda to greet them,

and at the sight of her Poppy's heart sank. She wasn't quite sure what she had expected, someone vaguely mannish perhaps, or plain and dedicated, but Astrid was neither of these. Petite and blonde, she had her hair cut short to emphasise the icy perfection of her features, and she wore a deceptively simple black dress that contrived to look cool and sophisticated, and yet practical at the same time. Obviously Astrid's administrative skills weren't all that Keir admired about her, Poppy thought sourly.

'Keir!' Astrid smiled at him possessively. 'Welcome back!' Her pale blue eyes swept over Poppy, who was certain that she could see the string holding up the shorts. 'You must be Penelope.'

'Poppy,' Keir corrected her almost curtly. 'Poppy, this is Astrid Lewis, as you've no doubt gathered.'

The two women nodded at each other with a marked lack of enthusiasm. Poppy felt clumsy and crumpled next to Astrid's petite perfection.

Guy Williams rose to his feet as Astrid ushered them inside. With his wavy hair, deep brown eyes and warm smile, he was far better looking than Keir, who was looking boot-faced as Poppy returned Guy's smile. Here at least was a friendly face. His easy manner reminded her of Ryan Saunders. She realised with an odd feeling of guilt that she hadn't mentioned her meeting with Ryan that morning. Well, there hadn't really been an appropriate moment... Poppy shrugged the feeling aside. She didn't have to account to Keir Traherne for everyone she met!

'Isn't that your shirt, Keir?' Astrid asked in a sharp voice.

Does she think I've stolen it? wondered Poppy acidly. 'My bags were lost on the flight out,' she said. 'I've had to borrow this from Keir while Gabriel washes my clothes.'

'What a nuisance!' Astrid looked at Keir sympathetically. Poppy had no doubt that she was the nuisance referred to.

Keir frowned. 'It's more than a nuisance. We're going to have to kit her out completely before she can go into the forest. She can hardly trot out to Camp One like that.'

'Haven't you got anything else?' Astrid turned to Poppy, thin brows raised.

'No. Just what I wore out.'

'I always travel with a couple of spare outfits in my hand luggage.' Astrid gave Poppy a condescending smile. 'When you've travelled around Africa as much as I have, you learn never to trust the airlines.'

'I'm afraid I'm not that organised,' Poppy confessed.

'The words "Poppy" and "organised" are mutually exclusive,' Keir added in a scathing tone to Guy.

Astrid looked smug. 'Never mind, you'll learn. And I'm sure we'll be able to find you something to wear.' She cast a cold eye over the generous lines of Poppy's figure. 'Mind you, you're quite a bit bigger than me...' She trailed off meaningfully.

Poppy clenched her teeth. Accepting a drink gratefully from Guy, she offered Astrid a bright smile. 'I know, I *am* quite tall, but it's not usually a disadvantage. I like to be able to look people in the eye.'

'You're welcome to borrow anything of mine you need, Poppy.' Guy was admiring the long legs, appealing curves and wide green eyes. 'Just say the word.'

'That's nice of you, Guy.' Poppy smiled at him and wondered why Keir was looking so disapproving. 'To tell the truth, I don't really know what it is I do need. My explorer kit only ran to a couple of pairs of shorts and a Swiss Army penknife!'

Guy grinned, but Astrid took her literally. 'You wouldn't get very far in the rain forest with that!' Her smile was calculated to remind Keir that he was lucky he had at least one person around who knew what she was doing.

CHAPTER FOUR

KEIR was watching Poppy. 'We'll just have to manage. I'm sure that between us we can lend her everything she needs,' he said shortly. 'She doesn't need to look like a fashion plate.'

'Shall I take Poppy out with me when I go to Camp One on Tuesday?' Guy asked quickly, with a glance at her mutinous expression.

'That sounds a good idea.' Astrid gave Poppy a cold blue look.

Keir frowned. 'Poppy can come with me. I want you to chase up those export permits, Guy.'

'I'd much rather show Poppy the jungle,' said Guy, disappointed.

'I've no doubt you would. But, knowing Poppy's propensity for disasters, I'd feel safer if she was where I can keep an eye on her.'

'When were you thinking of going out to the camps, Keir?' Astrid asked. 'If you go on Monday I could come with you ... and perhaps give Poppy a few tips.'

Poppy's heart sank, but to her relief Keir shook his head. 'I want to leave tomorrow, and I'll need you to be here to man the radio while Guy's away.'

'Of course.' Astrid was obviously torn between satisfaction at knowing herself indispensable and annoyance that Poppy was going to have Keir to herself.

Not that she needed to worry, Poppy thought. Keir would hardly be interested in a scruffy nuisance like herself when he knew that the glamorous, efficient Astrid was waiting for him.

'Isn't tomorrow a bit soon to drag Poppy out?' Guy was asking. 'The poor girl must be exhausted.'

'This isn't a holiday camp,' Keir said shortly.

'I don't mind,' Poppy said, still grateful that she wasn't going to have Astrid as company. 'As long as we don't have to leave in the middle of the night again.'

'Five o'clock isn't the middle of the night,' Keir said irritably. 'But tomorrow we'll leave in the afternoon—that ought to give even you time to wake up and get ready.'

'In the afternoon?' Astrid echoed. 'You won't make it to the camp before dark.'

'Poppy's not acclimatised. We'll take it in easy stages and spend the night on the trail. Even so, you'll find it hard going, Poppy. You're not used to walking in this kind of heat.' He looked pointedly at her drink. 'I'd advise you not to drink too much tonight. You'll suffer for it tomorrow.'

Astrid's nod of knowing agreement was enough to make Poppy drain her glass defiantly and hold it out to Guy for a refill. Meeting Keir's eyes, she wondered for a moment if she saw a glimmer of amusement there, but when she looked again it had gone and been replaced by a more familiar pained expression.

She noticed that Astrid soon manoeuvred the conversation round to business so that Keir was forced to give his attention to her and Poppy was free to bask in Guy's undemanding company. The warm admiration in his eyes was so different to Keir's habitually exasperated expression that Poppy began to feel quite exhilarated and they were soon enjoying a light-hearted flirtation. Out of the corner of her eye she could see a muscle beginning to twitch in Keir's temple and, although he continued to listen to Astrid, Poppy could tell that he disapproved. Crossing her long legs, she gave Guy a warm smile and had the satisfaction of seeing the twitch deepen.

'You know, you're not a bit as Keir described you,' said Guy.

'Really? What did he say?'

Guy hesitated, then grinned. 'He said you were the most infuriating female he'd ever come across.'

That sounded like Keir! Poppy sniffed. She glanced over at Keir again and leant forward confidentially. 'Why is he so anti women? Was he jilted at the altar or something?'

'Not that I know of!' Guy chuckled. 'I wouldn't have thought Keir was the type to languish with a broken heart anyway,' he said, unconsciously endorsing Poppy's own opinion. 'He'd probably just think that waiting till the last moment to jilt him showed a lack of organisation and forethought!'

'Then why is he so prejudiced against women?'

Guy looked thoughtful. 'It's probably because he had a bad experience on the last expedition he organised, in Zaire. It was a similar sort of set-up to this one, but not so big. Well, there was a nurse and a female botanist at one of the camps, and between them they stirred everyone up. They were the sort of girls who thrive on tension and that camp always had an "atmosphere"—it's hard to describe, but it wasn't very pleasant. There was a lot of jealousy, and as a result nobody worked very well together. Keir had to try and sort everything out and cope with the girls' whingeing the whole time—why couldn't they have a separate washing area, the men were making sexist jokes, it was too hot and too dirty, on and on! Personally I think it was just a personality problem, but Keir vowed he would never have women on an expedition again.'

'I must be infuriating if I'm worse than those two,' Poppy pointed out, affronted.

Guy shifted uncomfortably. 'Oh, well, I don't think he really meant it. He's got a few problems on his plate at the moment, especially with this new development deal threatening the project. Did he tell you about that?' When Poppy nodded, Guy went on grimly, 'Ryan Saunders has a lot to answer for!'

'Ryan Saunders?'

Guy didn't seem to notice the note of astonishment in Poppy's voice. 'He's the bloke with the so-called development scheme—quite a scheme it is too. Chop down the rain forest, make a lot of money and leave the whole world worse off. It's ironic really that it's precisely the kind of exploitation that our research is aimed at preventing.'

It was hard to believe that the Ryan Saunders who had chatted to her so pleasantly that morning was the arch-villain of the development scheme, but Poppy decided that this was not the time to mention that she had met him in Mbuka. She had a feeling it was unlikely to go down well with Keir, and she had enough black marks against her already. Instead she smiled at Guy and teased, 'So it's not just me making Keir so grumpy?'

'He has been a bit abrupt since you arrived,' Guy admitted, adding loyally, 'But normally he's a great bloke. He's got a mind like a steel trap, but he never talks down to people and he can be good company. The scientists here respect him because he's outstanding in his field, but probably more because he gets things done. That's no mean feat somewhere like this.' Guy paused and looked over to where Keir was looking thoughtful at something Astrid had said. 'Of course, he's not a man who suffers fools gladly.'

'He's certainly not suffering me gladly,' she said in a gloomy voice. 'How come Astrid doesn't get labelled a trouble-making woman?'

'Keir's worked with her in the past. She's a perfectionist like him and he knows he can rely on her—I suspect she's too valuable to him for him to worry about her sex, and, anyway, she never gets involved with any of the men.'

Too busy trying to get involved with Keir, Poppy thought bitchily. Glancing over at him now, she was in time to see Keir lift his head and smile at Astrid. It was the smile that so transformed the thin, intelligent face, and her heart twisted with an unexpected jealousy. She turned back to Guy abruptly with a bright smile. 'Enough about him. Tell me about you, Guy.'

Glad to oblige, Guy kept her amused with stories of his first trip to Africa and in return she told him about being arrested that morning. Guy laughed

about her struggles to dredge up some French and
the more she told him, the more she began to laugh
too. 'I must have looked such a sight, sitting there
covered in mud, gaily claiming to be Keir's wife!'

Astrid's ears must have been on stalks, for at that
she called over sharply, 'What are you two giggling
about?'

Guy wiped his eyes. 'Poppy was just telling me
about her first brush with the police this morning.'

'It's not funny,' Keir said repressively. He gave
Astrid a terse account of what had happened, and
she clicked her tongue.

'Really, Poppy, didn't you think? I know that
I've spent enough time in Africa to be very wary
of the police, but I'd have thought anyone would
have had enough sense not to wander around
snapping pictures like a tourist in London. Heaven
only knows what Henri must think about the
project now. Keir's quite right; that kind of thing's
not funny.'

'No.' Having got the giggles, Poppy was finding
it difficult to stop. Keir shook his head, but the
creases at either side of his mouth deepened and
eventually he gave in and laughed too.

The meal was immaculately presented, rather like
Astrid herself, thought Poppy, but rather bland.
Astrid, no doubt feeling that Poppy stood in need
of some instruction, devoted herself to passing on
the benefit of her years of experience of Africa,
until Poppy knocked over her glass and was able
to change the direction of the conversation.

Afterwards, much to her relief, Astrid trans-
ferred her attention back to Keir, making a deter-

mined attempt to monopolise him till he stood up abruptly. 'Poppy's looking tired. She'd better go to bed.'

Poppy looked up in surprise. She was tired, but she hadn't thought it showed.

'I'll walk her back if you want to talk business,' Guy offered quickly.

'That won't be necessary. I'll go with her.'

Astrid followed up Guy's lead. 'We really ought to talk about how we're going to approach MESRES about those new permits,' she reminded Keir.

'We can do it tomorrow morning.' Keir's tone was curt to the point of rudeness. 'Come along, Poppy.'

Meekly Poppy followed him out on to the track. He walked quickly, as if he were annoyed, and she had to struggle to keep up.

'Do you think you could slow down a bit?' she gasped. 'You're the one who said I was looking tired.'

Keir reduced his pace reluctantly, but didn't say anything as they walked together. He walked with his hands thrust into his pockets and looked at the ground. Poppy looked at the ground too, but she was very conscious of the decisive lines of his body in the dim moonlight.

At the bottom of the veranda steps, Keir paused.

'I know that Guy can be very charming, but I'd be glad if you didn't encourage him too much,' he said in a cold voice. 'He's got a lot of work to do and he doesn't need any distractions at the moment.'

Poppy gaped at him. 'Encourage him? What on earth do you mean?'

'You know what I mean, Poppy. All those long legs and giggles. You were flirting with him all evening.'

'I was not flirting,' she lied indignantly. 'I'm sorry if my legs were on show, but if it had worried you that much you could have lent me some trousers, and I was laughing because Guy was good company, which is more than you and Astrid were.'

'Astrid is very pleasant company.'

'To you, perhaps. *Yes, Keir, no, Keir, of course you're right, Keir.*' Poppy mimicked Astrid's tone wickedly. 'How can you bear someone who agrees with everything you say? She did nothing but patronise me all evening!'

'Don't be ridiculous!'

'I'm not being ridiculous, Keir! If I hear one more word about how long she's spent in Africa and how much she knows about Africa and how I don't know anything about Africa——'

'You *don't* know anything about Africa,' Keir put in in a glacial tone. 'It's not Astrid's fault she's had different experience from you—although sometimes I wonder just what experience you do have.'

Poppy ignored his last comment. 'No, it's not her fault, but she doesn't have to bang on about it the whole time. I'm sure Guy's had just as much experience, but at least he showed some interest in me.'

'In you, or in your big green eyes? Guy's too much a man not to have been distracted more by those legs of yours.'

'Unlike you, I suppose?' Angrily, Poppy turned to the steps, but he put out an arm to bar her way.

'I'm a man too, Poppy,' he said softly.

Suddenly he was standing very close to her. Poppy's heart began to thud painfully and she backed until she came up against the veranda. A shower of bougainvillaea petals fell on to her shoulder. She swallowed. 'In that case, I'll try not to distract either of you.'

Keir reached out and brushed the petals off her shoulder, and then his hand slid slowly, almost thoughtfully to her waist to pull her close to him. 'I think you're going to find that rather difficult,' he said. His other hand lightly brushed the curls away from her face.

Poppy stared up into his face as if spellbound by his touch. She could feel his hand warm against her back; the strong fingers drifting from her hair left her tingling and weak-kneed with desire. Instinctively her own hands went to his chest.

With a smothered oath, Keir jerked her closer, and bent to capture her mouth with his own. His lips were cool against hers and she opened herself to him as he explored her mouth with his tongue, his hands insistent against her spine. Poppy was enveloped in a hazy excitement. Nothing mattered but the feel of him, the touch of him. Her fingers spread against his chest and his kiss deepened, became more urgent in response to her own helpless, leaping desire.

And then, quite suddenly, he released her.

Poppy almost fell back against the veranda, thankful for its support. In the darkness, Keir's eyes were unreadable.

'I'm a man too,' he said again, 'and you, Penelope, are the distracting type.'

Poppy stopped and shifted the rucksack on her shoulders once more. She was panting hard and the hair clung to her neck and forehead, damp with sweat. Wiping her upper lip with her arm, she gazed resentfully after Keir. Despite the enormous pack on his back, he moved with easy, economical movements along the narrow trail. They had only been walking a couple of hours, and already Poppy was exhausted.

She had somehow expected the rain forest to be flat, but since they left Adouaba she seemed to have spent the whole time either toiling up steep hills, or slithering down the other side, only to be faced with yet another agonising climb. Neither seemed to affect Keir's steady pace.

'You didn't tell me there were going to be hills,' she shouted after Keir's back.

'You didn't ask.' Keir was in a bad mood today. He hadn't referred to the kiss they had shared last night, and in the clear morning light Poppy had found it hard to believe it had happened at all. But the memory of his hands against her skin, his lips against her throat, the strength of his chest beneath her fingers, was too vivid to be denied.

Poppy had stood beneath the bougainvillaea long after Keir had gone inside, trying to calm her whirling senses. She was unsettled, almost frightened by the way she had responded to Keir's kiss. She had never reacted with such abandon before. Keir's last words had been so dispassionate that he had clearly not been moved at all.

Uneasily she remembered what Guy had told her about Keir's experience with troublesome women. Did Keir think she was going to be like that, flirting with one man, kissing another? Was he just testing to see how she would react? If he was, he might well think she was going to be just as troublesome as he'd predicted, Poppy reflected. He wasn't to know that she had only flirted with Guy to annoy him. He would think she would kiss any man in the dark, she realised, surprised at how desolate she felt at the idea.

She hugged her arms together as if to comfort herself. She had never been kissed quite like that before—it was humiliating to think that it hadn't meant anything at all to Keir. Perhaps he *was* attracted to her? It seemed unlikely, given that he disapproved of her so strongly, but if it was true he would certainly resist getting involved. She was only here for a short time; he wouldn't bother wasting his time pursuing a purely physical attraction. He would probably think of the kiss as a momentary lapse of concentration, Poppy thought bitterly, kicking at the petals at her feet. For him it would have been a moment's impulse, and he would be regretting it already.

Keir's brusqueness the next morning had seemed to confirm this, and Poppy's battered pride responded in kind. If he wasn't going to refer to last night, neither would she. Let him think it hadn't meant anything to her either. Don't let him think for a minute that she had lain awake half the night, wondering...

She had been rather proud of her air of unconcern over breakfast, but still she had been unable to prevent her heart lurching later that morning when he strode into the house, his arms full of borrowed equipment for her.

Poppy had gazed in dismay at the pile of mosquito nets, hammock, plastic sheeting, water bottles and boxes of dehydrated rations. 'I'll never be able to carry all that!'

'It's half what Astrid carries,' Keir had said unfairly, but it was enough to ensure that Poppy hoisted the pack on to her shoulders without further comment.

In spite of the crushing weight, Poppy was fascinated by her first sight of the rain forest. On either side of the path the tangled vegetation pressed, green and glossy. Above them, the light filtered through the forest canopy, broken every now and then by a clearing where a shaft of sunlight drove through the dimness.

Poppy tilted her head back to peer upwards whenever she heard the shrill cry of a bird or the flurry of leaves as some creature moved about the canopy, but the growth was so dense and intertwined with creepers that she could see nothing except a still swaying branch or the swing of a drooping liana.

She walked with her eyes on the forest, intrigued by the sense of teeming life hidden in the greenness while all that was visible was the butterflies flitting along the path or the trails of tireless ants. The path was narrow and gnarled with roots: Poppy kept tripping over them to sprawl on the ground, incapable of getting up with the unaccustomed weight on her back until Keir retraced his steps impatiently to set her on her feet again.

'For heaven's sake,' he said the third time it happened, 'why can't you look where you're going?'

'I was watching that butterfly.' Poppy pointed to a huge butterfly with electric blue wings that flapped slowly between the light and the shadows. 'Isn't it beautiful?'

'Ah, yes.' Keir glanced at it and reeled off a scientific name in Latin that meant nothing to Poppy. They stood and watched the butterfly's languid progress together.

'I must take a picture!'

They both became aware at the same time that Keir was still holding Poppy's arm, and he released it hurriedly. 'There isn't time now.' As Poppy opened her mouth to protest, he went on, 'They're very common and you'll see plenty later on. If you spend any more time falling over we won't even make it to the camp tonight, so do you think you could do a little less dreaming and a little more watching where you're putting your feet?'

Resigned, Poppy trudged after him, envying his firm tread as he ducked beneath overhanging branches or slashed at the undergrowth that spilled out on to the path with his machete. He stepped easily over fallen trees that barred their way while Poppy scrambled awkwardly behind him. Once she exclaimed in delight when the path went right through the hollow trunk of an enormous tree, and it took a good deal of cajoling before Keir would allow her to unpack her camera and take a photograph.

'We may as well have a rest here while we're at it,' he said, shrugging off his pack.

Poppy collapsed untidily on to a nearby log with a sigh of relief. Keir, unscrewing the top of his water bottle, eyed her with disapproval. She knew that he was probably comparing her unfavourably with Astrid's neatness, but she didn't care. The hated rucksack was off her back and that was all that mattered.

'You'd better have some water before you de-hydrate.' Keir eyed Poppy's red face critically and handed her the bottle. She drank greedily, tipping her head back and letting the water splash over her face.

'That's the best thing I've ever tasted,' she said at last, handing back the bottle with a smile. 'Who needs champagne?'

Keir found himself smiling back as he sat beside her on the log. Rummaging in one of the pockets of his pack, he produced a grapefruit and peeled it with deft fingers. He handed Poppy half and they sat eating it in silence, listening to the sounds of the forest all around them. The grapefruit was sweet and juicy, and as Poppy bit into a segment the juice dribbled down her chin. Catching the drop with her middle finger, she sucked it thoughtfully, her eyes still on the majestic tree straddling the path.

She turned to ask the name of the tree and the words dried in her throat. Keir was watching her, and there was something in the light grey eyes that held her captive, her finger still at her lips. The jungle that had so fascinated her seemed to fade into insignificance as she stared back at him as if mesmerised, trying to read his expression but conscious only of a slow fuse burning within her that spread an insidious warmth through her body.

Suddenly, the canopy above them erupted into life. There was a squawk and a flurry of activity in the canopy. Startled, Keir jerked his gaze upwards, then back to Poppy, then hurriedly back to the canopy.

'Red colobus monkeys,' he said in a gruff voice. His high cheekbones were tinged with the faintest of flushes.

Poppy forced her attention to where he was pointing, high in the branches. 'How can you tell? I can't see anything!'

Keir unslung a pair of binoculars from round his neck. 'It's quite rare to see them in this area. Here...' He passed her the binoculars, and Poppy felt her skin tingle where his fingers brushed against hers. 'Now, see that swaying branch? Go up a bit and to the right, no, up a bit more——'

'I see them!' Poppy broke in, glad of the excuse to concentrate on something other than the lean body so close to hers. As she watched, one of the troop of monkeys leapt from his branch, landing effortlessly in the next tree before swinging onwards. After a moment's hesitation, the others followed, and suddenly the canopy was full of monkeys leaping in breathtaking acrobatics from tree to tree.

Poppy lowered the binoculars as the last of them disappeared into the treetops, her face livid with delight. 'Oh, weren't they wonderful?'

Keir nodded, but his eyes were on her face rather than the canopy. With the passing of the troop, an uncanny silence seemed to have fallen on the forest, only the last swaying branches bearing witness to the fact that they had been there at all. Poppy glanced at Keir, but he had turned abruptly away. 'We'd better get on.'

Lifting up her pack, he held it out so that she could slip into the straps easily. Poppy couldn't help grimacing as the weight pulled down her back and Keir frowned. He walked round to buckle her belt at the front, and then adjusted the shoulder-straps while Poppy watched his hands. Strong, capable hands with long fingers and characteristically neat, square nails.

'Is that better?' he asked brusquely, and she nodded, suddenly, stupidly, shy.

She stumbled less as they walked on, her eyes on her feet and her mind busy with her own thoughts. He hadn't touched her—all he had done was look at her with cool grey eyes—but it was as if he had kissed her all over again. If he had made any move towards her, she would have melted into his arms...

Poppy stared down at the ground, dismayed at the way her thoughts were leading her. It was stupid to read too much into a mere look, too much into a casual kiss, two brief moments set against the fact that the rest of the time he clearly found her exasperating. As far as he was concerned, the sooner she left, the better, and she would do well to remember it. She had a job to do, and when it was done she would leave. There was absolutely no point in getting involved with Keir Traherne. Pull yourself together, she told herself sternly.

By the time they stopped for the night, Poppy had talked herself into renewed confidence. Perhaps she was attracted to Keir, but it was purely physical, and more than likely it was merely a result of finding herself in such an alien environment where he was the only familiar figure. Poppy ruminated over this idea. It seemed to make sense, and saved her pride. She was tired as well, she reminded herself. No wonder she was reacting strangely.

She must reassure Keir that she wasn't stupid enough to misread the situation. She was here purely as a photographer, and from now on she was going to be a professional. She would be cool and capable, dignified. She wouldn't argue; she would keep her mind on the job and off Dr Traherne. Unconsciously, Poppy straightened her shoulders.

Keir had stopped in a small clearing. A stream ran nearby and a charred circle on the ground showed that they were not the first to stop here.

'The local hunters use this as a camp sometimes,' Keir said. 'We'll spend the night here and go on to Camp One tomorrow morning.'

Poppy struggled out of her pack and flopped down on top of it, giddy with relief that they had stopped at last. She watched as Keir put up a shelter with a deft efficiency that she could only admire, hanging up two hammocks and draping mosquito nets over them from a higher branch.

'It's not going to rain, is it?' Poppy asked, as he fixed up a plastic sheet to cover everything.

'It's unlikely to. This is still the dry season, but the rains could start any day now and, knowing your luck, I wouldn't be at all surprised if it was the one night we're sleeping in the open!' When Poppy looked rueful he took pity on her and added, 'I always sleep under a cover in any case—it keeps the worst of the dew off.'

He lit a fire and squatted beside it, feeding the flames with one hand and mixing dehydrated food and water in a mess tin with the other. His energy made Poppy feel even more weary, but she roused herself to ask if she could do anything to help.

Keir glanced up at her tired face in time to see her smother a yawn. 'You could stir this while I go and refill the water bottles,' he said in a gruff voice.

Obediently, Poppy took the mess tin and stirred the unappetising-looking mixture. Goodness only knew what it was supposed to be. She picked up the packet: chicken supreme. Wrinkling her nose, she tossed the packet on to the fire. It didn't look like any chicken supreme she had ever had!

The tropical darkness was closing in with alarming speed. It seemed as if the forest was coming alive around her, with a cacophony of buzzing, sawing, whirring, squeaking and rasping, and Poppy bent to put another piece of wood on the fire, annoyed with herself at the way her heart had begun to thud apprehensively. What was Keir doing? It couldn't take all this time to fill up a few water bottles, surely? She bit her lip and glanced around the clearing. There must be all sorts of creatures out there, lurking. What if something had happened to Keir?

All at once there was a rustling in the undergrowth. Poppy jumped to her feet, knocking the mess tin on to the ground as her hand went to her throat. The next instant Keir emerged. He was whistling cheerfully and she subsided, feeling foolish.

Cool, calm, dignified, *remember?*

Quickly she scooped the spilt 'chicken supreme' back into the tin. A little bit of dirt wouldn't do them any harm.

'All right?'

'Fine,' Poppy said brightly. She watched him as he hunkered down by the fire. He looked so comfortable, so at one with his surroundings, that one glance at the tough line of his cheek lit up by the flickering flame, or the strong hands clasped loosely between his knees, was enough to send her fears scuttling back into the darkness.

Poppy felt herself relax in the security of his presence. She even enjoyed the chicken supreme, although Keir inspected it suspiciously after a couple of mouthfuls.

'This tastes a bit odd...'

Poppy retrieved a piece of twig surreptitiously from her own plate, glad that Keir couldn't see her clearly. 'Tastes fine to me.' She changed the subject quickly. 'I've never been anywhere like this before,' she said, gesturing about her. 'It's sort of frightening, isn't it?'

'Frightening?' Keir looked across at her in surprise. 'I think it's fascinating! Just think of all those millions and millions of organisms around you.'

'That's exactly what I am thinking of!'

'But that's not frightening! They all exist together in one complex system. Everything has its place in the order of things. You might think it looks chaotic, but it's not at all.' He pushed the mess in his tin around with his fork reflectively. 'I think that's why the forest appeals to me so much. Even as a small boy, I liked the idea that there was an order to everything. I used to spend hours classifying beetles! I suppose I'm still doing much the same thing,' he went on with a wry smile. 'I know people say I'm a perfectionist, and a workaholic, but the truth is that I find details fascinating. I just like the thought of everything fitting together neatly. It's like doing a jigsaw; every time we find something out, it's another piece slotted into the picture. In the end, if we're lucky, we might have a clear idea of exactly how it all works.'

Poppy looked at the fire, thinking of Keir as a small, serious boy poring over his beetle collection. She felt strangely intimate, as if he had dropped his guard and allowed her a rare glimpse of the man behind the façade of brusque efficiency.

'I suppose you think it all sounds very boring,' Keir was saying.

'No.' She shook her head. 'It's never boring finding out what makes people tick. It's just so different from the way I go about things.'

'Is there *any* order in your chaos?' he asked, with a trace of amusement.

She sighed. 'I wish there was.' It would be nice to have someone ordered and dependable, a rock she could cling to when the muddle threatened to overwhelm her. Firmly she pushed the thought aside. 'I do try to sort myself out, but I never seem to quite manage it.'

'You seem to have done quite well in spite of it all,' Keir remarked. 'Not many photographers your age would be working for a company like Thorpe Halliwell.'

'That was just an accident. I started out doing wedding photos, portraits of children and pampered pets, that kind of thing.' She grimaced at the memory. 'I only got the Thorpe Halliwell job by running over the managing director of one of their subsidiaries.'

'Rather a drastic way to go about getting a job,' Keir commented in a dry voice.

'I didn't do it deliberately! I was on my way to photograph some ghastly poodle, and I was late—of course—and I suppose I wasn't really looking. Fortunately he wasn't hurt, and I must say he was absolutely charming about it. We got talking, he asked to see my portfolio and things sort of went on from there. I met Don Jones through him, and that's how I'm here now. My career hasn't exactly followed a logical progression!' It hadn't been logical, but, retelling it, Poppy found herself feeling as if every mistake, every clumsy accident, had led to this moment, to her sitting alone in the firelight with Keir.

'I'd have been surprised if anything about you had been logical!' Keir said. 'Tell me, are your relationships as muddled as the rest of your life?'

'I suppose so.' She sighed. 'You wouldn't believe how complicated things can get sometimes! I always seem to get landed with all the dreary men—and if they're not dreary they want me to be a sister to them!'

Keir raised an eyebrow. 'Why bother with them?'

'Oh, I don't know...I suppose I'm not very good at saying no.' She broke off, realising how Keir might misconstrue what she had said. 'I mean, I'm too soft-hearted to say no when they ask me out.'

'I know what you meant,' Keir said drily.

They shared a mug of tea in silence, gazing into the dying embers of the fire, each wrapped in his or her own thoughts. Poppy wished she hadn't told Keir about her unexciting boyfriends; she should have pretended that she had a whole queue of dynamic, glamorous men waiting to sweep her off her feet, so that he wouldn't think there was any chance of her being impressed by *him*!

CHAPTER FIVE

THE silence was interrupted by the ominous rumble of thunder overhead. Keir looked at Poppy accusingly as the first heavy drops of rain splashed on to their hands.

'What are you looking at me like that for?' she demanded, indignant. 'It's not my fault it's raining!'

Keir merely snorted. 'Come on, we'd better get under shelter.'

'I don't suppose it ever rains when Astrid's camping out,' Poppy said waspishly as she climbed awkwardly into her hammock.

The rain crashed down on to the flimsy plastic covering and poured over the edge to splatter noisily on the rubber sheet Keir had spread out beneath them. It was so loud that they had to shout to make themselves heard. Poppy lay rigid, unused to the rocking motion of the hammock whenever she moved. The temperature had dropped dramatically with the rain. Earlier that day she had wondered if she would ever feel cold again; now she shivered beneath the cotton sleep sheet Astrid had lent her.

Keir had been packing away the remains of the meal and now swung himself easily into the hammock next to hers. 'Cold?'

'A bit.' Poppy gritted her teeth to stop them chattering.

'Astrid gave you a sweatshirt, didn't she? Put that on.'

'I left it behind. There seemed so much to put in my pack, and I never dreamt I'd need it.'

'Astrid wouldn't have given it to you if you didn't need it,' Keir said in exasperation.

Poppy looked sulky. 'I thought it was supposed to be hot in the tropics!'

'It is. It's just the contrast that makes it feel cold.' Keir looked over at her again and sighed irritably. 'You'd better climb in next to me. Body heat's the best thing when you're cold.'

'It's all right,' Poppy said.

'Don't be ridiculous, woman. You're shivering, and I'm not going to be able to sleep with your teeth going like castanets a few inches from my ear.'

Biting her lip, Poppy sat up gingerly. The hammock lurched as she wriggled out of the sleep sheet, and when she tried to disentangle herself from the mosquito net it abandoned the struggle and dumped her unceremoniously on the ground. Winded, Poppy lay sprawled on the plastic while the rain splashed down her neck from the sheet above.

'Poppy!' Keir covered his eyes with his hand and counted to ten as she picked herself up, humiliated. 'Come on.' He patted the side of his hammock and, through the exasperation, Poppy thought she detected a smile in his voice.

Rather shyly, she clambered in beside him. The hammock rocked alarmingly. 'Careful!' he said with more than a touch of asperity. 'We'll both be on the ground if you don't watch out!'

None the less, he lifted his arm invitingly and Poppy slipped beneath it to rest her head against the solid warmth of his chest. His arm closed round her shoulders and he shifted slightly in the narrow hammock until she fitted snugly against the length of his body.

Her teeth were still chattering, and he rubbed his hand up and down her arm until the shivering began to subside into treacherous enjoyment. 'You really are cold, aren't you?'

What had happened to her resolution to remain coolly professional? Where was the competent photographer who had vowed to keep Keir Traherne at a businesslike arm's length? Poppy knew that she should have stayed independently in her own hammock, but it felt so safe and warm in his arms.

She could hear the steady, reassuring beat of his heart beneath his shirt as she relaxed into him, and her arms crept tentatively round him. His breathing was deep and regular, his chest rising and falling in time with her own. He rested his chin on her soft curls, and at last his other arm covered hers so that she was wrapped tightly to him.

Poppy drifted into sleep, cocooned in warmth. Later she was never sure how much she dreamt, but at one point she thought she felt his lips against her hair, and when she murmured his name sleepily his arms tightened in reassurance.

Poppy was very impressed with the scientists' camp, which seemed at once part of the forest and the epitome of twentieth-century efficiency.

'Keir built the camp for us before we arrived,' Alan Patterson explained to Poppy as he showed her round. 'He's a remarkable bloke. It takes a lot to set up a project like this and he did it practically single-handed.'

Alan was a lepidopterist, and very enthusiastic about the set-up. 'This is where we do all the cooking,' he said, pointing out a long bamboo table covered by a bright blue tarpaulin. A couple of gas burners stood on one end and a selection of black and battered saucepans hung from the bamboo frame. Rough wooden tables and benches had been made for the eating area, and more tarpaulins covered raised sleeping platforms.

The pride of the camp, though, were the scientific laboratories, which had been constructed inside a row of tents. High benches made of the inevitable bamboo were covered in instruments and specimen jars and, incongruously, a selection of computers donated by Thorpe Halliwell.

'We've got a generator which gets switched on at certain times,' Alan said in reply to Poppy's puzzled expression. 'All mod cons, as you can see. It's not surprising that scientists are clamouring to get on a project run by Keir Traherne.'

Poppy soon got sick of hearing Keir's praises sung, particularly as he seemed to be ignoring her, and had hardly spoken to her since their arrival. She had been rather shy after spending the night snuggled in his arms, but Keir had been brisk and practical as ever the next morning. He might as well have slept with a sack of potatoes for all the effect it had on him, Poppy thought bitterly.

In defence she pursued her resolution to be strictly professional and made a great effort not to notice what Keir was doing. Fortunately, she had plenty to keep her occupied, photographing the scientists at the computers or studying specimens and ensuring that the Thorpe Halliwell logo was always cunningly located somewhere unexpected. These photographic sessions were always the source of much amusement, and whenever Keir found Poppy she seemed to be surrounded by a laughing group of men.

'Why are you always so disruptive?' he demanded, finding her alone for once. 'You're not here to entertain the troops, you're here to take photographs. Surely it doesn't require every single man in the camp standing around with a fatuous expression on his face as well?'

Poppy put down the lens she had been cleaning and looked at him. 'I don't think that's very fair. They're just glad of some company. Just because you don't want to talk to me, it doesn't mean that nobody else does either.'

'It's not a question of not wanting to talk to you.' Keir frowned irritably and slapped at a blackfly. 'I've got a job to do here—as have all the other men—and only a limited amount of time. In case you didn't notice the other night, the rains are starting, and we need to get the bulk of the work finished as soon as possible. What we don't need is you distracting everybody.'

'I suppose Astrid doesn't distract anybody when she comes out?' Poppy picked up the lens again and rubbed it crossly.

'No, she doesn't. She just gets on with her job with the minimum of fuss. A concept apparently alien to you.'

Turning on his heel, Keir strode off. Poppy made a face at his retreating back. She was glad Alan and John Wyatt were taking her with them the next day—the less time she spent with Keir Traherne, the better!

She enjoyed being with Alan and John and walking through the forest without the weight of the pack on her back, but somehow it wasn't the same without Keir. It was the first time she had been away from him since she arrived in Cameroon and it was a shock to discover just how used she was to listening out for his crisp, decisive tones or to watching out of the corner of her eye for a glimpse of his dark, austere features.

Poppy was pleased with the shots she got that day, including one of John casually holding a gaboon viper. Tired but happy, they got back to camp just as it was getting dark.

Keir glowered at John. 'You said you'd be back two hours ago!'

'We went a bit further than we intended,' John replied mildly. 'We thought Poppy would like to see the view from that plug of volcanic rock.'

'Poppy!' Keir exploded. 'I might have known Poppy was behind it. I'm glad she's got so much energy, because she's got to walk back to Adouaba tomorrow. I can't waste any more time showing her the *view*!'

'He's been prowling around like a bear with a sore head all day,' one of the botanists confided as

Keir stomped off. 'And when Chris commented on how quiet it seemed without Poppy he just about bit his head off.' He grinned reassuringly at Poppy. 'He doesn't usually make a fuss when we're late. I think he must have something on his mind.'

'Not much doubt what it is, either!' John threw a teasing glance at Poppy, but she didn't notice.

'No,' she agreed absently, watching Keir's receding back. Now that she had seen the project in action, she had a better idea of what was at stake, and she felt a wave of sympathy for Keir in spite of his abruptness. The logistics of organising a camp like this would be headache enough, but he also had the responsibility of trying to fight off Ryan Saunders's proposals for the future of the forest. No wonder he was preoccupied!

Deaf to pleas for Poppy to stay a little longer, Keir marched her out of camp early the next morning.

'I want to get back to Adouaba today. It's a long walk, but provided you don't waste time dawdling we should be able to do it easily.'

He set a punishing pace and Poppy had soon forgotten how much she'd missed him on the previous day's walk. She plodded after him, muttering about forced marches. She had expected her pack to be lighter this time, after leaving all their spare rations with the scientists, but instead Keir had insisted that they weigh themselves down with specimens which had to be catalogued in Adouaba. They had only been walking an hour, and already her shoulders ached, her neck ached and she could feel her shoes beginning to rub ominously against her heels.

Keir allowed her one brief break. Poppy, her sympathetic understanding of his problems quite forgotten in the struggle to keep up, was feeling mutinous, and determined to make the most of it by getting out her camera.

'What are you doing?' he asked sharply.

'What does it look like?'

'We haven't time——' Keir began, but Poppy interrupted him.

'Last time you promised there'd be masses of these butterflies about, but this is the first one I've seen since, and I am *not* moving on until I've got a picture, so you'll just have to wait.'

Keir restrained himself with an effort. 'Oh, very well,' he said through clenched teeth. 'But don't take too long.'

Poppy spent long minutes setting up the photograph while Keir fretted in the background.

'For heaven's sake!' he burst out as she changed her lens yet again and began to focus it. 'Why can't you just take the picture? By the time you do all that the bloody thing will have flown away.'

'It will if you keep shouting like that,' Poppy whispered fiercely. 'And stop pacing around—you'll frighten it off.'

'It's all a ridiculous waste of time,' he grumbled, but withdrew to stand fulminating by the packs.

Patiently, Poppy stalked the butterfly with her camera and was rewarded by the perfect shot as it settled with the sunlight on its wings.

'If you've quite finished now,' said Keir icily, 'perhaps we could get on? Or would you like to spend another hour taking that beetle there?'

'Where?' Poppy looked round with interest.

'Never mind—just hurry up!'

'You're always in such a rush,' said Poppy, putting her camera away with slow deliberation, just to annoy. 'I think you must be a closet commuter. Why don't you give all this up and go home where you can spend your time worrying about being in time for the six-fifteen from Waterloo? I'm sure you'd be much happier there.'

'And why don't *you* just shut up and get a move on?' Keir retorted, nettled.

Why was he always so grumpy? Poppy glowered at his back as he strode ahead of her. She had found herself liking him more and more on the way out to the camp, but since the night they had sat and talked by the fire he had been even more irritable than before. So what if he had things on his mind? There was no reason for him to shout at her, or pretend she didn't exist just because she was being polite to the others!

Poppy stomped onwards, rehearsing arguments as to why Keir Traherne was the most unreasonable, intolerant, downright unpleasant man she had ever come across, but as the hours wore on even that enjoyable diversion wasn't enough to take her mind off her feet. Her shoes were rubbing her heels and soles raw and her fingers had swollen like sausages until only force of will kept her going.

The blisters were agonising, every step a torture, but she was determined not to give Keir the satisfaction of pointing out how unfit she was. Poppy was quite sure that Astrid never got blisters. Biting her lip to stop from crying out, she trudged slowly onwards.

Her head was bent and she was concentrating so hard on putting one foot in front of another that she walked slap into Keir, who had stopped to wait for her with an impatient expression.

'Poppy!' He put out a hand to steady her, and then his voice changed suddenly. 'Why are you walking like that? Blisters?' Tilting her chin, he looked down into her glazed eyes.

Poppy nodded dumbly.

'Let me see.' He shrugged off his pack easily and made her sit down on it. Then he knelt and took off her trainers. Her feet were covered in blisters, red-raw and ugly, and she winced as he touched them gently.

'Why didn't you say something?' Keir sat back on his heels and looked up into her face.

Poppy shrugged helplessly. She was trying not to cry. 'I thought you were in a hurry,' she said at last in a small voice.

'We could have gone a lot quicker if you'd told me about these before.' In spite of his gruff voice, Keir's expression was gentle. He pulled a first-aid kit out of his pack and covered the worst of the blisters with zinc oxide tape.

'It's not ideal, but it's the best I can do for now, I'm afraid. Have a rest before you put your shoes back on again.' He rummaged in yet another pocket of his pack and produced some boiled sweets. 'Here, have one of these—they're good for your glucose levels.' He unwrapped one for her and popped it in her mouth as she opened her lips obediently. The comforting homeliness of the gesture made her eyes suddenly sting with tears.

Keir sat down on the ground next to her and looked at her slumped shoulders. 'Poor Poppy; I've been pushing you too hard, haven't I?'

Poppy looked up quickly at the unexpected note of contrition in his voice. 'I'm afraid you're not used to having someone like me holding you up.'

He concentrated on unwrapping a sweet for himself. 'No, I've never come across anyone like you before, I must admit.' He pleated the sweet wrapper very carefully and put it back into the pocket. 'But I should have made allowances for the fact that this is all new to you. I'm sorry. I'm not normally like this.' He smiled. 'You seem to bring out the worst in me for some reason.'

Poppy wished that Keir wouldn't smile like that just when she had convinced herself what an objectionable person he was. It was such an unexpected smile, a wickedly attractive grin full of a light-hearted charm that belied his austere exterior. As before, Poppy felt her antagonism dissolve. What was it about this man that had her swinging wildly between hostile resentment and treacherous attraction? She could lecture herself all she liked on remaining cool and neutral; it still only took one smile from Keir to expose it as mere wishful thinking.

'I've been difficult too,' she muttered now.

'Very,' Keir agreed cheerfully. 'Perhaps we should both try harder?'

Poppy was unable to resist smiling back, and for a moment her feet were forgotten. 'Perhaps we should.'

'I don't like to do this to you, but we've still some way to go.' He stood up and put out a hand to haul her to her feet. His fingers were strong and cool against hers and Poppy had an almost irresistible impulse to cling on to them. Keir gave her hand a little squeeze and then dropped it.

'How are the feet?'

'Well...' Poppy tested them gingerly. 'They're still feet, I suppose.'

She reached out for her pack, but Keir forestalled her. 'I'll take that. You just concentrate on walking.'

'You can't take my pack as well as your own!' Poppy stared at him, appalled.

'Why not?' He finished buckling on his own pack and swung hers up to balance on his head as easily as if it had been empty. 'You go first.'

It was certainly easier without the weight on her pack, but even so Poppy became more and more silent. Her feet no longer felt like feet; they felt like savaged lumps of meat, and she began to feel lightheaded with the excruciating pain that came with every step. She could never have done it without Keir's constant encouragement, but her spirit nearly broke when darkness began to fall and with it the rain. They were resting for a few minutes, and Poppy's face was screwed up with the effort of not crying. *I won't cry, I won't cry, I won't cry.* The words circled hypnotically round her weary brain.

'We're only about half an hour from home,' Keir said. 'I could carry you from here. I'll leave the packs under a bush and collect them tomorrow.'

'No.' Poppy drew a shuddering breath. 'I've walked this far, and I'm going to walk all the way. All the way into my bedroom.'

'Good girl.' Keir's smile gleaming through the dusk was reward enough.

Never had a house appeared more welcoming. Gabriel had switched on the lights and they beckoned tantalisingly through the rain as Keir and Poppy made their weary way along the track at last. Both of them were soaked by the time Poppy dragged herself up the veranda steps. Groping her way to one of the bamboo chairs, she collapsed into it and for long moments could do nothing more than gaze blankly ahead of her, her green eyes huge in her white, strained face. Her whole body buzzed with exhaustion while little rivulets from her wet hair ran unheeded down her nose.

Keir let her sit while he got rid of the packs and explained the situation to Gabriel in rapid pidgin. Then he fetched a towel and ruthlessly rubbed Poppy's hair, ignoring her muffled protests.

When she finally emerged from the towel, her hair stood up in a fluffy halo and her eyes were bright once more. She rubbed her ear tenderly. 'Did you have to be so rough?'

'Don't talk nonsense,' Keir said briskly. He used the towel to mop up the last drips from her face and neck before handing her a huge glass of whisky. 'Here, drink this.'

'I don't really like whisky.' Poppy wrinkled her nose, but Keir was implacable.

'Drink it anyway. It'll do you good.'

She took a cautious sip, then another as Keir stood over her. Despite her show of coughing and spluttering, the spreading warmth in her stomach was welcome, and she drank some more gratefully.

Satisfied that she could be trusted to drink by herself, Keir sat down opposite her, leaning his elbows on his knees and staring at his own glass which he twirled thoughtfully between his hands. His wet shirt clung to him, emphasising the strength of the body underneath. Poppy couldn't see his eyes, could only see the firm line of his nose and the angular cheekbones. A lock of wet hair fell over his forehead. Something in the way he sat, so compact and self-contained, made her heart turn over.

Suddenly he looked up and caught her watching him. As always, the light grey eyes were startlingly unexpected against his dark features. Poppy felt as if she had never seen him before. Everything about him seemed extraordinarily clear and definite: the dark hairs on his forearms, the pulse in his throat, the creases at the edges of his eyes. She wanted to reach out and touch him.

It was very quiet in the room, although the rain continued to crash down on to the roof and in the background the generator throbbed to itself.

Keir smiled and Poppy felt dizzy happiness seep through her as she smiled back.

I love you.

The realisation rang like a bell in her heart. It was so clear, so obvious, that for one horrified moment Poppy wondered if she had spoken it aloud, but there was no reaction on Keir's face as he resumed his study of his whisky.

'How do you feel now?'

Exhilarated, blissful, enchanted, in love. 'Fine,' said Poppy, shocked at how husky her voice sounded.

'In that case, I suggest you have a hot shower, and then I'll dress your feet for you. Can you bear to stand up again?'

She got stiffly to her feet, wincing as her blisters screamed in protest. Her legs were trembling, whether from exhaustion or Keir's hand at her elbow she wasn't sure.

'Will you be able to manage, or would you like a hand?' His eyes glinted as they reached the bathroom door.

'I can manage,' she croaked, but as she stood under the shower, trying to distribute her weight away from her blisters, she couldn't help wondering what it would be like if Keir were there with his strong, gentle hands. A slow flush spread over her body as she imagined him soaping her...

'Stop it!' Appalled, Poppy shook herself free of her drifting imagination. She must get a grip on herself. It was too late now to deny that she loved him or to pretend that it was mere physical attraction. It was as if in the one sudden moment of revelation everything had fallen into place, and her own reactions were all blindingly obvious.

Four Irresistible
Temptations
FREE!

PLUS A MYSTERY GIFT

Temptations offer you all the age-old passion and tenderness of romance, now experienced through very contemporary relationships.

And to introduce to you this powerful and highly charged series, we'll send you **four Temptation romances** absolutely **FREE** when you complete and return this card.

We're so confident that you'll enjoy Temptations that we'll also reserve a subscription to our Reader Service, for you; which means that you'll enjoy...

FOUR BRAND NEW NOVELS - sent direct to you each month (before they're available in the shops).

FREE POSTAGE AND PACKING - we pay all the extras.

FREE MONTHLY NEWSLETTER - packed with special offers, competitions, authors news and much more...

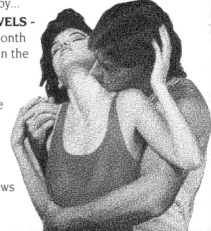

Free Books Certificate

YES! Please send me **four FREE Temptations** together with my **FREE gifts.** Please also reserve a special Reader Service subscription for me. If I decide to subscribe, I will receive four Temptation romances each month for just £6.60 postage and packing free. If I decide not to subscribe I shall write to you within 10 days. The free books and gifts are mine to keep in any case. **I understand that I am under no obligation whatsoever.** I may cancel or suspend my subscription at any time simply by writing to you. I am over 18 years of age.

A Free Gift

Return this card now and we'll send you this cuddly Teddy Bear absolutely FREE together with...

A Mystery Gift

We all love mysteries, so as well as the FREE Teddy Bear there's an intriguing FREE gift specially for you.

MS/MRS/MISS/MR _____

ADDRESS _____

_____

_____ POSTCODE _____

12A1T

MILLS & BOON
FREEPOST
P.O. BOX 236
CROYDON
CR9 9EL

Offer expires 31st May 1992. The right is reserved to refuse an application and change the terms of this offer. Readers overseas and in Eire please send for details. Southern Africa write to Book Services International Ltd, P.O. Box 41654, Craighall, Transvaal 2024. You may be mailed with offers from other reputable companies as a result of this

NO
STAMP
NEEDED

mps

Unfortunately Keir's feelings were *not* obvious. Nothing about Keir was obvious, Poppy reflected with a sigh as she dried herself.

As she hobbled out of the bathroom, still wrapped in a towel, Keir appeared in the doorway of his room. He had stripped off his wet shirt, and Poppy had to make an effort to drag her gaze away from his bare chest.

'I've put a dry shirt and a sarong on your bed. I'll have a quick shower myself and then dress those feet for you.'

She could hear him whistling in the shower while she dressed. The shirt and the sarong knotted round her waist were comfortable, but hardly very elegant, and suddenly she longed for something attractive to wear, something that would make Keir notice her as a woman and not as a nuisance.

'You're the distracting type.' He had said that after he had kissed her that night. But Keir Traherne wasn't a man who wanted distractions, she reminded herself sternly. He wanted a peaceful, orderly life with a girl like Astrid who would never contradict, irritate or distract him.

Her whisky was still sitting by the chair and she gulped at it, overcome by a wave of desolation at the thought of Keir and Astrid together.

'You're supposed to savour whisky, not toss it back like a Cossack!' Keir's voice sounded amused from behind her as she spluttered at the whisky's burning effect.

Poppy turned, her eyes smarting. Trust him to catch her looking ridiculous! As usual, he looked neat and decisive, and not at all like a man who had walked all day carrying two packs.

'Sit down and I'll do your feet for you. How are they now?'

'Sore,' Poppy admitted, still coughing, and sat obediently where he indicated. Keir sat cross-legged on the floor in front of her and took her feet gently in his hands. Poppy shivered at his touch and he looked up in quick concern.

'Still cold? Surely not after all that whisky!'

'No,' she said, and then, when he looked puzzled, 'I just . . . shivered, that's all.' She looked down at him defiantly.

Keir lifted an eyebrow, but didn't comment. He pulled over a plastic bowl of water and ordered her to put her feet in it. 'It's just salt water,' he said.

Poppy lowered her feet in gingerly and immediately took them out again with a yelp as the salt stung her blisters. 'Ouch!'

'Come on, don't make a fuss!' Keir pushed her knees down firmly. 'Leave them there for a couple of minutes.'

She rolled her eyes and grimaced but he was unimpressed. 'There's worse to come,' he warned. After what seemed to Poppy an age, he spread a soft towel on his knees and lifted out her feet. She watched him as he patted them dry almost tenderly. Or was that wishful thinking?

'Am I ever going to walk again, Doctor?' she asked in a mock-feeble voice.

Keir looked up as his hands slid to her ankles. His thumbs massaged them thoughtfully. 'After today, I'm surprised that you want to even think about walking again.'

'I'd have enjoyed it if it hadn't been for my rotten feet.'

'Next time we'll take preventative measures.' To Poppy's disappointment he stopped rubbing her ankles and went back to drying her toes. 'But we're not going anywhere for a few days until these have healed.' He picked up a small can. 'This is going to hurt, I'm afraid.'

'Oh.' Poppy eyed it warily. 'What is it?'

'Iodine.' Holding her foot firmly, Keir sprayed the yellow liquid directly on to the blisters. Poppy nearly went through the roof. When he had finished, her eyes were watering and she could only gasp like a landed fish, but it was worth it when he ruffled her curls. 'Well done.'

'I'm sorry if I've thrown out your plans,' she apologised, when she could speak.

'If I've learnt anything since you arrived, Penelope, it's been to not make any plans at all while you're around, as any sensible, logical arrangement would undoubtedly be doomed to failure!'

Poppy hung her head. 'I'm sorry,' she said again. 'Guy told me what trouble you had with those two women on the last expedition. I didn't want to be like them.'

'You're not like them.' Something in his voice made Poppy lift her head to look at him questioningly. 'You're a different kind of trouble,' he added reflectively. 'A quite different kind of trouble!'

Poppy's mouth felt dry. His words might be critical, but the light in his eyes set her blood pounding with hope. When he stooped suddenly to lift her in his arms, hope flared into incredulous anticipation.

'What are you doing?' she whispered.

'I'm taking you to bed.' Their eyes were very close as green stared into cool grey. 'So that you can rest your feet,' he explained softly. 'I know you vowed you'd walk all the way to bed yourself, but you can think of this as a lap of honour.'

It wasn't what she had allowed herself to hope, but as he laid her on the bed and closed the door softly behind him Poppy was hardly aware of her aching feet.

He could pretend to be as brusque and efficient as he liked; the long, painful walk home had showed her a kind, considerate man beneath the façade. A man with unexpectedly gentle hands. A man with a smile that turned her bones to water. A man who just might not be quite as indifferent as he pretended either... Poppy wriggled into a more comfortable position and settled herself for sleep, warmed by the memory of the look in his eyes. Her feet throbbed painfully, but she would willingly have walked another day just to see him look at her like that again.

CHAPTER SIX

ASTRID looked disapproving the next morning when she saw Poppy sitting on the veranda with her feet propped up.

'I thought Keir was supposed to be taking you to Camp Three today?' The blonde girl was wearing a sleeveless khaki shirt and matching trousers with a webbing belt. She looked immaculate, Poppy thought gloomily, wondering how she avoided creasing her trousers. Perhaps she never sat down.

'We were, but I've sent Guy instead.' To Poppy's relief, Keir appeared in the doorway and answered Astrid's question for her. 'Poppy can't walk anywhere at the moment.'

'Can't walk?' Astrid looked at Poppy accusingly. 'Why on earth not?'

'Er—blisters,' said Poppy. Astrid always made her feel about six years old.

'Blisters!' Astrid's scorn was obvious. 'Don't tell me you're going to let a few blisters put you off?'

Keir frowned. 'It's more than a few blisters. Her feet are in an appalling mess and I don't want her walking anywhere for the next day or so.' Poppy saw Astrid's eyes narrow at the unconsciously proprietorial note in his voice as he went on, 'In any case, there's more than enough to keep me busy here. I'm going to try and finish off that report for

101

the ministry. We don't want Ryan Saunders getting in ahead of us.'

Taken up with her feelings for Keir, Poppy had forgotten all about Ryan Saunders. Watching the grim look on Keir's face, she was glad she hadn't mentioned her brief meeting with him. 'You're right, of course, Keir.' As usual, Astrid was quick to agree with him. 'It just seems a pity for Penelope to waste her time sitting around when she's got such a short time out here.'

'The sooner her feet heal, the sooner she can get out to the other camps,' Keir said shortly.

And the sooner we can pack her off home, Poppy added to herself bleakly.

Astrid was obviously thinking the same thing. 'Perhaps Guy could take her out when he gets back?' she suggested. 'Then you could finish your report in peace.' She glanced meaningfully at Poppy, who lifted her chin and glared back.

'We'll see.' Keir looked non-committal.

'Anyway, I must get on.' Astrid resumed her brisk manner. 'We can't all afford to sit around all day. I'm going to see about renewing those visas, then I'll work out a resupply list for the camps and finish typing out John's report.' She looked smugly at Poppy, a model of efficiency and reliability.

She really was unbearable, Poppy thought indignantly, watching Astrid bustle off. Couldn't Keir see how ghastly she was?

He was gazing after Astrid reflectively. 'Useful woman,' was all he said, and then glanced down at Poppy with something like irritation. 'I've got a lot of work to do today, so I'd appreciate it if you'd just stay here. I don't want to hear you or see you and you are not, repeat *not* to walk around on those feet. Is that clear?'

'Perhaps you'd better give it to me in writing, just to be sure,' Poppy said, nettled at being treated like a naughty child.

'Judging by your behaviour in Mbuka, I've no reason to believe you'll simply do as you're asked, as anyone else would,' Keir retorted.

'You won't even know I'm here,' she said loftily.

Half an hour later there was a crash. Startled, Keir looked up from his computer to see Poppy staring guiltily down at the table she had knocked over behind him. Her contorted creeping hobble was a long way from the noiseless slink she had intended.

'What do you think you're doing?' he demanded in an ominous tone.

Poppy set the table upright and bent to gather the papers that had been carefully laid out on top of it. Thank goodness nothing was broken! 'Well...I thought it wouldn't disturb you if I just slipped in to find a book to read.'

'Is that what you call just slipping in? A herd of elephants stampeding through here would have disturbed me less!'

'I'm sorry, but I...oops!' The papers slipped out of her hands and scattered on the floor. Keir's chair scraped back angrily.

'For heaven's sake, leave them alone! You've done enough damage as it is!' He snatched the few remaining sheets from her hands.

'I'm sorry,' Poppy said humbly. 'I didn't mean to disturb you.'

Keir glanced up from where he crouched on the floor, sorting the papers into neat piles. As always when she looked into his eyes, Poppy felt a tiny, thrilling jolt, but his expression was exasperated, almost bitter.

'No, I don't suppose you did mean to,' he said heavily, 'but you do anyway. There must be about forty or fifty people involved in this project, and together they aren't as disturbing as you!'

Poppy bit her lip. 'I'm sorry,' she said again. 'I know you don't want any distractions.'

There was a tiny pause, then Keir said, 'No.' He ran his hands through his hair. 'And what are you doing on your feet?' he glowered, as if he'd suddenly remembered why he was angry. 'I thought I told you to stay on the veranda?'

'I will—as soon as I've got a book.'

Keir gave up. He sighed and shook his head as he turned back to his desk. Taking his silence as agreement, Poppy hobbled over to the bookshelves and ran her finger along the spines. Most of his books were a little too highbrow for her, she thought ruefully, longing for a good pot-boiler. At this rate she would be forced to improve her mind.

She was pulling out *A History of West Africa* without much enthusiasm when her eye was caught by a familiar name. *Trees of the Tropical Rain Forest* by K.D.K. Traherne.

'Is this you?'

Keir glanced up from his computer and grunted an acknowledgment. Poppy flicked through the pages. It was beautifully illustrated with glossy photographs which appealed to her professional eye. She turned it over thoughtfully and studied the photo of Keir on the jacket cover. He looked younger, but the cool intelligence of the grey eyes was the same.

'I didn't know you were a world authority on tropical trees!' she read off the cover.

Keir wore severe horn-rimmed glasses when he was reading. He took them off now and rubbed the bridge of his nose wearily. 'That was when I was able to work undisturbed.'

'What does D.K. stand for?'

'What?'

'It says K.D.K. Traherne. I wondered what the D and the K stood for.'

'David Knighton. Now would you please shut up and let me get on with some work?'

Poppy would have liked to have asked more. Why David? Why Knighton? She knew nothing about his family or where he came from. She wanted to know everything there was to know about him; all she knew was that she loved him. But Keir's expression as she opened her mouth to ask the questions that bubbled to her tongue warned her against pushing her luck too far, and she retired to the veranda instead.

She found his book surprisingly readable and was impressed by the spare economy of his writing, but her attention kept wandering back to Keir. She could see the back of his bent head through the window. He sat still and concentrated, absorbed in his work. Poppy chewed her lip as she watched him.

If only she had that ability to shut everything out and concentrate absolutely on what she was doing. Perhaps her life wouldn't be quite so haphazard and perhaps—perhaps—Keir might learn to love her too.

While Keir worked, Poppy daydreamed. In her dream she had transformed herself miraculously into someone practical but feminine, dedicated yet sophisticated, skilful yet modest. It was a combination Keir would be unable to resist. He would sweep her off her feet, demand that she remain as his assistant and——

Here Poppy's dream broke off abruptly. Keir already had an assistant who was everything that she was not, she reminded herself bleakly, and she would be a fool to forget it.

'Where do you think you're going?'

Poppy, attempting to creep out quietly without disturbing Keir, froze in the doorway. Did he have eyes in the back of his head?

'Oh, just out,' she said airily.

Keir looked suspicious. 'Out where, exactly?'

'Gabriel said he'd take me to the market.'

'He did, did he?' Keir frowned over the top of his glasses. 'You're supposed to be resting your feet.'

'They're so much better, though, Keir. Really they are, and I'll go mad if I have to sit still any longer!' Poppy smiled cajolingly. 'It's only to the market—hardly a jungle trek!'

'Hmm.' He sounded unconvinced, but he picked up his pen again. 'If your feet are that much better, I'd better take you to the chief this afternoon.'

'Not the police again?' Poppy exclaimed in dismay.

Keir looked amused. 'No, not the police—unless you're planning on some outrageous escapade in the market. Nesoah is the tribal chief in this area. He'll certainly know you're here; he'll probably know about your blisters. I wouldn't be surprised if he even knew how many times I've wanted to strangle you since you arrived!'

I wonder if he knows that I'm in love with you? Poppy turned away abruptly, afraid the involuntary thought would show in her face.

'If he knows all about me, why does he want to see me?'

'If he knows all about you, he probably doesn't,' Keir pointed out in a dry voice. 'But it's courtesy to introduce a stranger, so we'd better go along. The chief's an important man round here and we need to have him on our side. He'll represent the local people, and his opinion could make all the difference to whether the minister decides to let us carry on or not. Perhaps you could try and remember that you're representing the project when you meet him?'

He eyed her disparagingly. Her white trousers were hopelessly grubby again, and somehow she had torn her shirt. Poppy sighed.

'Perhaps I should go and buy something else to wear in the market? Will the chief expect me to be very smart?'

'This isn't Paris—presentable should be enough of a challenge for you.'

Poppy enjoyed her morning in the market, a smaller and more intimate version of the one in Mbuka. It was hard for one of her sunny temperament to stay downcast for long, and the noise and colourful activity of the market were enough to lift her spirits. She was soon on the friendliest of terms with the stall-holders and, mindful of her reason for being there in the first place, took a whole reel of film before persuading Gabriel to come and bargain for a traditional-looking outfit in bright greens and yellows. Chanel it wasn't, but she longed for something different to wear and the vibrantly patterned material had caught her eye at once.

Delighted with the price Gabriel had haggled for her, Poppy counted out some grubby notes while the stall-holder wrapped the outfit carefully in newspaper and tied it with a piece of frayed plastic string. She walked home, swinging her parcel gaily from one finger, and chatting and laughing with Gabriel. Neither of them understood half of what the other was saying, but it didn't seem to matter.

Keir was still immersed in his computer when she got back, so Poppy tiptoed across the room behind him, heading for her bedroom.

'I don't know why you're bothering to be quiet now,' Keir said grumpily, without turning round. 'I could hear you and Gabriel shrieking all along the road. What was so amusing?'

'Oh, I don't know,' Poppy said cheerfully. 'We were just enjoying ourselves.'

'Well, could you just try and enjoy yourself quietly from now on?'

Poppy made a face at his back and escaped to her room. Why was he always so grumpy with her? Why did one half of her bristle with indignation while the other half longed simply to slip her arms round him and kiss the cross lines away from his face?

She pondered the problem as she tried on her new outfit. She had always imagined that when she fell in love it would be with someone perfect. Someone who thought *she* was perfect. Poppy sighed. Nothing could have been further from the truth. Never in a million years would Keir think she was perfect: the idea was so absurd that she had to smile. But then, he was hardly perfect either. He was brusque and bad-tempered. He was neat and pernickety. He was intolerant and infuriating. He wasn't even handsome.

It was just that the mere thought of him was enough to make her heart turn over.

Poppy turned slowly in front of the mirror. If only she could convince herself that it was merely a physical attraction. If it had been Ryan Saunders, she could have understood it more. He was a good-looking man, much better looking that Keir. Poppy screwed up her eyes in an effort of memory, but couldn't quite recall Ryan's features. She could visualise every line of Keir's face, as clearly as if he were standing in front of her.

Memory would soon be all she would have of him, she thought.

Poppy tried desperately to concentrate on her outfit. There was no point in getting gloomy, she chided herself. There had been times, especially after that awful walk, when she could have sworn that Keir almost liked her. Perhaps if she was quiet and unobtrusive over the next few days, Keir might begin to view her differently?

She eyed her reflection with a sinking heart. If she wanted to be quiet and unobtrusive, she couldn't have chosen a worse outfit. Flamboyant was the word that sprang to mind. Keir was going to hate it.

Still, it was too late now, and she didn't have anything else. Rather nervously, Poppy presented herself to Keir after lunch, braced for his scathing comments.

For a moment he didn't say anything. He just looked at the way the vivid material emphasised her tall, slender figure, and deepened the green of her eyes. 'Unusual,' he said at last, and then he smiled. 'Funnily enough, it quite suits you.'

The chief's house was a simple wooden structure. An immense, grizzled man, he greeted Keir jovially and eyed Poppy with interest. Keir's smile and grudging compliment had been enough to make her glow with happiness and now she beamed back at the chief as they shook hands, her own swallowed up by his massive paw. It was dark inside the hut, but as her eyes adjusted she could see that it was simply furnished with wooden benches and that the floor, though mud, was swept clean and dry.

Gesturing for Keir and Poppy to sit, the chief shouted and a younger man appeared with a bottle and some grubby glasses.

'What's this?' Poppy whispered to Keir, as she accepted a glass of the cloudy, pinkish liquid somewhat dubiously.

'It's palm wine,' he said out of the corner of his mouth. 'The chief will be offended if you refuse, but for heaven's sake don't drink too much of it.'

It smelt vile. Poppy took a cautious sip, relieved to discover that it didn't taste quite as bad as it smelt. Gradually the hut filled up with men who drifted in to join in the conversation. Keir seemed to know most of them, and she found herself wishing that he smiled at her that easily. His white face and pale blue shirt stuck out a mile, and yet he looked relaxed and at home.

A wave of longing washed over her so unexpectedly that Poppy gave an involuntary gasp. Almost as if he had heard it above the hubbub, Keir looked up, and their eyes met across the room for a brief moment before she turned away and took a slug of the palm wine. Feeling his eyes upon her, she fumbled for her camera, desperate for him not to see the naked desire on her face.

'May I take your photograph?' She stood in front of the chief, who grinned, and posed obligingly. After that, of course, she had to take pictures of everyone and at the chief's insistence posed with him while Keir watched with a resigned expression.

Glasses were filled and refilled. The hut throbbed with voices. Poppy was beginning to feel peculiar but, finding herself the centre of attention, felt

unable to refuse as yet more palm wine was pressed
on her. It no longer seemed to matter that she
couldn't speak pidgin. She was getting on famously
with the chief and both laughed uproariously at
each other's incomprehensible jokes.

Keir was standing over her. 'I think it's time I
took you home.'

'I was just going to have some more wine.' Poppy
gazed owlishly down into her glass.

'You've had more than enough already.' Keir re-
moved the glass firmly from her grasp and pulled
her to her feet. 'Say goodbye to the chief.'

'Goodbye to the chief.' Poppy giggled and then
caught herself guiltily on a hiccup.

After the dim interior of the hut, the heat and
light outside hit her like a slap in the face. Poppy
screwed up her face against the glare and swayed
uncertainly.

'I feel sick.'

Keir was unsympathetic. 'I'm not surprised. That
palm wine's lethal. I told you not to drink too much
of it, but would you listen?'

'I was just being polite.' Poppy concentrated on
walking to the Land Rover in a straight line.

'Polite? Ha!' Keir held the door open for her with
obvious sarcasm. 'Just making an exhibition of
yourself more like!'

'I wasn't!' she cried, spoiling the effect with
another hiccup. This made her giggle again, and
this time she couldn't stop. In the end, Keir had to
bundle her into the vehicle where she flopped,
helpless, over both seats.

'You're impossible,' he said, reluctant amusement warring with annoyance in his voice. He pushed her over so that he could climb in. 'You've obviously got no idea how to behave. How a reputable company like Thorpe Halliwell could have anything to do with you is quite beyond me!'

Slamming the Land Rover into gear, he set off along the bumpy track. The annoyance was obviously winning, Poppy thought. 'Was that supposed to be you on your best behaviour?' he went on. 'Was it too much to ask that just for once you could appear the sensible, professional photographer you claim to be?'

'I'm sure I never said I was sensible,' Poppy put in involuntarily.

'Do you need it spelt out in words of one syllable?' he asked furiously, ignoring her interruption and enunciating very slowly and clearly. 'You—must—give—the—right—impression,'

'Impression's got three syllables,' Poppy pointed out, trying to tear her eyes away from the hand changing gear so savagely.

Keir gritted his teeth. 'Can't you take anything seriously? Astrid's quite right; you're childish and irresponsible.'

'You've no right to discuss me with Astrid,' Poppy said with a touch of sullenness.

'I've got every right when you seem hell-bent on destroying every shred of reputation we've built up in this area! If you'd been specially recruited by Ryan Sanders, you couldn't have done more harm to the future of the project!'

'Rubbish!' Poppy said bravely, still buoyed up with palm wine.

'I've got a good mind to put you straight on a plane home!' Keir stamped on the brake as a goat ran into the road, and Poppy covered her face with her hands. 'Africa's no place for children,' he went on as if nothing had happened.

Poppy lowered her hands. 'I expect Astrid told you that.' The jolting over the holes in the road was making her feel even sicker. 'Astrid knows everything about Africa. She's spent years and years and years in Africa, you know.'

'That's enough, Poppy,' Keir said warningly. 'I don't think you'd better say any more until you've sobered up a bit.'

To Poppy's horror, Astrid was waiting on the veranda as they drove up. Elegant and obviously very much at home in Keir's house, she watched Poppy's unsteady progress with distaste.

'What on earth's the matter with *her*?'

'Poppy has been introduced to palm wine,' said Keir drily.

'I see.' Astrid looked down her perfectly shaped nose as Keir helped Poppy up the steps and into her room.

'I seem to spend my whole life helping you to bed,' he said severely, as he lifted her legs under the mosquito net, but there was that reluctant note of amusement in his voice once more.

Poppy rolled over. 'I want to die,' she said into her pillow.

'I'm afraid that on this occasion you will probably survive,' he said, pulling off her shoes and dropping them to the floor. 'As I will probably live to regret it.'

'Really, that girl's nothing but a nuisance,' Astrid pointed out in a carrying voice as Keir joined her on the veranda. 'She doesn't know the first thing about how to behave somewhere like this. It must have been very embarrassing for you to watch her getting drunk in front of the chief. What must he have thought?'

There was a pause. 'Well, he's not exactly a tee-totaller himself,' Keir said eventually. 'He and Poppy were as bad as each other. With any luck he'll have too much of hangover to remember much.' His voice, pitched much lower than Astrid's, still floated clearly through the open window of Poppy's room.

'Well, I don't know! You've said yourself, Keir, that we really can't afford to lose our reputation at this stage, especially not with the ministry's decision coming up. We could have done without Penelope Sharp, couldn't we?'

This met with silence, but Astrid was undeterred. 'And what *was* that ghastly thing she was wearing?' she went on with her light, silvery laugh. 'I could hardly believe my eyes when I saw her! Those bright fabrics are all very well for the locals, but not for Europeans. She obviously doesn't have any kind of dress sense.'

'She lost her bags,' Keir pointed out, a slight chill to his voice. 'It's hard to buy anything else here.'

Poppy turned on her back to stare at the ceiling, puzzled by his unexpected defence. She could hear his footsteps moving across the veranda, and imagined him leaning on the rail. 'I thought she looked...' He trailed off into a silence. Poppy strained to hear more, but in the end all he said was, 'She's got the sort of personality that can carry off an unusual outfit.'

'It was certainly unusual!' Astrid sounded put out and, despite her thumping head, Poppy allowed herself a slow smile. Keir's defence had been almost grudging, but it was enough for her still to be smiling—albeit rather blearily—as she fell asleep.

CHAPTER SEVEN

POPPY woke the next morning with a chastening headache. Throwing back the mosquito net, she wrapped a sarong carelessly round her and padded to the window. Outside, the air smelt damp and rich and warm, and the insects had already embarked on another day of frenetic activity. It must be later than she thought.

A tiny, translucent gecko darted along the windowsill and disappeared into a crack in the wall as Poppy watched it.

'Lucky gecko,' she murmured, turning to look for an aspirin. Her memories of the previous day were blurred, but she knew she would have to apologise to Keir, and disappearing into a wall seemed like a much better idea.

Still, better to get it over with. She remembered him telling her that she was childish and irresponsible, and she bit her lip as she thought of her resolve to be quiet and unobtrusive. That hadn't lasted long! She would try harder this time, she really would. Sensible—that would be her new watchword.

Keir was at his usual position at his desk, bent over a report. The back of his head was peculiarly familiar, she realised, as if she had known him for years instead of just days.

Before she could say anything, Keir glanced over his shoulder and saw her standing uncertainly by the door. Astonishingly, his expression lightened, and, without thinking, she smiled, the warm, natural smile that seemed so much part of her. Then she remembered that she was going to be sensible from now on and stopped smiling. He would only think she was being silly and feminine.

'Poppy.' Keir stood up, and there was a sudden awkward silence as they faced each other. He cleared his throat. 'How do you feel?'

'Ghastly,' Poppy admitted with disarming candour. 'How could you have stood by and let them force me to drink all that palm wine?'

'I'm afraid the army wasn't available yesterday afternoon. I imagine it would have taken at least their combined forces to have stopped you!'

'Oh, dear!' Poppy looked guilty. 'Well, I . . . I'm really sorry if I embarrassed you. I didn't mean to be any trouble.'

Unexpectedly, Keir grinned, the grin that set her heart doing wild handsprings. 'No more than usual. You and the chief drank the town out of palm wine and you took no notice whatsoever of anything I had to say, but apart from that you were your usual angelic self.'

Poppy tried to look apologetic, but his smile was irresistible, and she couldn't help smiling back at him.

'It doesn't sound too bad,' she said, relieved. 'I was expecting you still to be furious with me!'

'Fortunately for you,' said Keir in a dry voice, 'we've had some good news this morning while you were still sleeping off your hangover, so I'm feeling lenient.'

'Good news? What is it?'

'Astrid had a message over the radio from one of our contacts in the capital. He's had a tip off from the ministry that they're going to turn down Ryan Saunders's proposal and give us a licence to carry on the project.'

'Oh, that's wonderful news!' Poppy flung her arms round Keir in an exuberant hug, only to stop, suddenly excruciatingly aware of how close they were.

It was as if Keir realised at the same time, for his arms, which had automatically closed round her, dropped abruptly, and they disentangled with some awkwardness.

Keir cleared his throat, and turned away to adjust some papers on his desk into a neat pile.

Poppy put on a bright smile. 'We must celebrate!'

'It's a bit too early for that,' said Keir. 'I won't allow myself to celebrate until I've got the licence in my hand. I don't trust Saunders, and he could still turn things round.' He glanced at Poppy and relented. 'But it's very encouraging news, yes.'

'I feel so useless! And I've been holding you up with my wretched feet when there's so much you should have been doing!' Poppy gazed at him with remorse. 'Can't I least cook a special meal or something?'

Keir's expression softened slightly. 'Don't feel too bad about your feet. In a way it's been a good thing having to stay at base for a bit. I've nearly finished this report, and once I've tied up the final details this should be what finally convinces the Minister that he's making the right decision.'

'You're just being nice,' Poppy accused him, uncertain of how to deal with this new, gentler Keir.

Keir smiled his heart-shaking smile again. 'If it makes you feel any better, I'll admit that I'd have been able to do twice as much if you hadn't been so damned distracting the whole time. Look,' he went on in a brisker voice, 'if you really do want to do something, perhaps you could cook a meal tonight? Gabriel's been asking if he can go back to his village for a couple of days, for yet another funeral. He seems to have an endless supply of relatives hovering at death's door, all ready to pop off conveniently whenever a feast comes around. Normally Astrid fixes up something instead, but she's going to be pretty busy too, so if you don't mind...'

Delighted to have something to do, Poppy rushed off to plan a wonderful meal for that evening. She had ascertained that Astrid wasn't likely to get back from the resupply run until later, so it would just be the two of them. Poppy's spirits soared. This would be her chance to show Keir that she wasn't quite as useless as he thought her.

She waved a beaming Gabriel off, and turned her attention to the kitchen, inspecting the contents of the store cupboard without enthusiasm. Tins of tuna and corned beef or packets of dehydrated spaghetti bolognese were uninspiring when she dreamt of producing some elaborate exotic concoction designed to astound Keir with her hitherto unsuspected culinary skills.

The pleasant daydream of Keir gasping in surprise and admiration lasted no more than a few minutes. Poppy was an enthusiastic but haphazard cook and experience warned her that in the kitchen, as elsewhere, any attempt to impress was doomed to failure. Regretfully she settled for chicken casserole and rice.

Simple but effective, she told herself as she made out a shopping-list. Surely even she couldn't go wrong with that?'

Why were things never easy? Poppy sighed to herself later that morning in the market. She was eyeing a flapping squawking bird which had been produced when she asked for chicken. Making herself understood without Gabriel was turning out to be rather more difficult than she had anticipated.

'No, I want a dead bird,' she tried to explain again.

At last, in desperation, she launched into a graphic mime, flapping her arms, clucking wildly and then drawing her finger across her throat before closing her eyes and letting her head drop to one side with a last dying squawk before her fascinated audience.

'Penelope! What *are* you doing?' Astrid's crisp tones cut across the laughter and jerked Poppy upright.

'I'm—er—trying to buy a chicken,' she said, feeling foolish.

'Buying a chicken has always been a relatively simple operation for me,' Astrid said acidly. 'I seem to manage it without making an exhibition of myself in the market.' She looked Poppy up and down patronisingly. 'I see you're not in national costume today!'

Poppy's eyes narrowed, but she decided not to rise to the bait. 'I was trying to make myself understood,' she said. 'I got as far as chicken, now all I want is a dead one.'

'I suppose you'd like it wrapped in a neat little plastic package too?' Astrid gave a condescending smile.

'That would be nice,' Poppy said in an even tone, longing to reach out and squash a tomato deliberately against Astrid's spotlessly clean shirt.

'You've no idea, have you?' Astrid gave a long-suffering sigh and spoke as if to a child. 'This is Africa. One can't afford to be squeamish. It doesn't take long for meat to go off in this heat. At least if it's running around, you know it's fresh.'

'Not being an old Africa hand, that hadn't occurred to me.'

'I'd have thought it was obvious. You know,' Astrid went on sweetly, 'if you took the trouble to think about things instead of rushing into embarrassing situations, you'd get on a lot better here. I know that Keir wishes you were a little less... exuberant.'

Poppy flushed, remembering her spontaneous hug that morning, and the way Keir had stepped quickly away. 'Shopping in the market isn't what I'd call an "embarrassing situation".'

'Not for you, perhaps, but I was certainly embarrassed to see the way you were carrying on. The

entire population of Adouaba probably thinks
we've got a lunatic working for us.'

'Rubbish!' Poppy said crossly.

'And after your performance at the chief's house
yesterday...' Astrid trailed off delicately. 'Well, let's
just say that you haven't done much for the project's professional reputation since you arrived.'

Poppy gritted her teeth. 'So you and Keir keep
telling me! I think you should wait to see my
photographs before you bang on any more about
being professional!'

'You mustn't take offence, Penelope. I'm only
trying to help. I know you haven't been to Africa
before, and things like going to the market must
be very strange to you.'

'It's not that strange!' Poppy snapped. 'You can
get yams in Sainsbury's now, you know.'

Astrid gave the irritating, tinkling laugh that set
Poppy's teeth on edge. 'I don't think it's quite the
same thing! Now, you don't seem to be getting very
far with this chicken, do you? Why don't you let
me sort it out for you?'

'No, thanks,' Poppy said shortly. 'I've decided
I don't want chicken after all.'

She walked slowly home, thinking about Astrid.
The other girl seemed determined to make Poppy
feel as if she didn't belong. Poppy was quite ready
to admit that she knew virtually nothing about
Africa, but the odd thing was that she *didn't* feel
all that out of place. She liked the untamed vegetation, the scruffy shops and the hot nights that
throbbed with jungle sounds. She liked the aimless
walk of the men, or the patient women with vast

loads balanced gracefully on their heads. She liked the bustling, vibrant markets and the bush taxis lurching alarmingly over the pot-holed roads.

She didn't want to go home and leave the colour and the chaos behind, any more than she wanted to say goodbye to Keir. She would have to, of course. Poppy thought of the future without Keir stretching emptily ahead of her and resolutely pushed it aside. She wasn't on the plane yet, and was determined to make the most of the time that was left. If she was very good, perhaps—*perhaps*—Keir would suggest that she stayed a little longer.

Her spirits rose at the dream, and she spent the afternoon pottering happily in the kitchen. In the absence of chicken, she was reduced to a fricassee made with tinned tuna, followed by pancakes as a celebratory gesture, but even this simple menu seemed to require the use of every dish in the kitchen, which soon looked as if a whirlwind of cooks had passed through, leaving a trail of dirty dishes, drifting vegetable peelings and spilt flour.

Oblivious to the mess, Poppy sang snatches from *The Sound of Music*, breaking off occasionally to scold herself for forgetting a vital ingredient or to stare in astonishment as yet another implement came apart in her hands. She was sifting flour for weevils when the door opened abruptly, and Keir strode in.

'I am *trying* to read a report on the finer points of soil analysis,' he pointed out heavily. 'But it's rather difficult to concentrate with Julie Andrews yodelling away in the background. It's taken me an hour to get through a page! Do you think you could shut up or at least sing in tune?'

'I didn't realise you could hear me,' Poppy apologised. 'The door was shut.'

'It would take a lot more than a door to shut you out, Penelope!' Keir glanced around the kitchen and sighed. 'I've always thought of cooking as a quiet, restful activity, but I can see that I was wrong. I find it hard to believe that anyone could make so much mess or so much noise making a simple meal. If it wasn't you squawking away about having confidence, it was pans clattering or china smashing. Is anything left in one piece?'

'I've only broken a couple of plates,' she protested.

'Oh? I distinctly heard more than two smashes!'

'Well, there was that mug with the broken handle,' Poppy admitted airily, 'but you won't miss that. I can't think why you have china anyway. Plastic's so much more practical.'

'Had I known how clumsy you were going to be, I'd have been to a Tupperware party before I came out,' Keir said in a caustic voice, but Poppy merely grinned.

'I'll clear it all up when I've finished. You'll never know that I was here at all!'

Keir looked at her, bright-eyed and dishevelled as she was in one of his old shirts and faded cut-off trousers. 'I doubt that, Poppy. I doubt that very much.' In spite of his dampening tone, there was an odd light in his eyes that set Poppy's heart beating in its now familiarly erratic pattern.

He reached out and wiped the flour off her nose and cheek with his thumb. 'You look a mess,' was all he said, but his touch was unexpectedly tender.

He closed the door behind him quietly. Poppy stood staring at it, struggling to bring her racing pulse under control. Her face burned where his fingers had brushed and she put a hand to her cheek as if to soothe it, while suppressed happiness seeped through her irresistibly.

'Oh, Poppy,' she murmured to herself, unable to wipe the idiotic smile off her face. 'If that's all it takes, you *are* in a bad way.'

The generator broke down in the middle of dinner.

'I didn't touch it,' Poppy said quickly.

Keir smiled his swift, disconcerting smile. 'For once, I believe you. It breaks down regularly.' He pushed back his chair and groped for the torch which stood on a shelf, ready for just such an emergency. 'I'd better go and have a look.'

Lighting Poppy a couple of candles, he left her alone in the flickering darkness, but he was back within a few minutes. 'There's nothing I can do about it until tomorrow. Damn! I wanted to finish the report tonight, too. Not much chance of that without the computer.'

He sat down again opposite Poppy. 'At least we don't need electricity to eat. We'll have to finish by candlelight.'

'Very romantic,' said Poppy lightly, and immediately wished she hadn't.

There was an awkward silence.

Idiot, she chided herself. She had been so aware of Keir after that brief encounter in the kitchen that she had become suddenly ridiculously shy of him. If Keir noticed her unusually tongue-tied state, he didn't comment, but carried on in so much his normal manner that gradually she had relaxed and they had been talking easily.

Now she had ruined it. Her flippant reference to romance seemed to reverberate between them in the enforced intimacy of candlelight. Across the table, Keir's eyes met hers, and she looked quickly away, desperate to find something, anything, to say to break the silence.

I love you. I love you. I love you. She could hardly say that.

She risked a glance over the table at Keir. His face was shadowed and remote. She pushed away her plate. Her appetite had gone.

It was Keir who spoke first. 'You're a good cook.' He sounded surprised, almost as surprised as Poppy was to hear the compliment. 'I wasn't sure what was going to emerge from all that mess, but it was delicious.'

Poppy fiddled with her glass. Being able to make pancakes wasn't much of a talent compared to Astrid's overwhelming competence, but it was better than nothing. 'I can't do much, but I can make a batter.' She tried to make a joke of it, but there was an note of bitterness in her voice, and Keir looked at her sharply.

'You can do more than that!'

'I can't think of anything else—except take photographs, of course.

'You can make people laugh.'

'That usually gets me into trouble.' Poppy sighed. 'I suppose Astrid told you about the market this morning.'

'She mentioned it, yes. I saw her just as she was leaving on the resupply run.' He hesitated. 'I gather it was quite a performance.'

'I bet she couldn't wait to rush along and tell you how I'd been disgracing the project's image again!' Poppy said sullenly. 'I was lectured in public as if I were a rather naughty schoolgirl.'

Keir gave a faint smile. 'Perhaps that's how she thinks of you.'

'Is that how *you* think of me?'

Poppy's abrupt question hung between them, echoing in the silence. She hadn't meant to blurt it out like that. Unable to meet his eyes, she watched a moth blunder towards the candle flame, and put out a hand to knock it gently away.

'No,' he said at last. 'I wish I did.'

The darkness was hot and heavy against her face. The ceiling fan must have stopped with the generator, Poppy realised inconsequentially. Outside, the insects shrilled even louder, as if in protest at the deep, still pool of quiet illuminated by the guttering candles.

Keir was watching her. Poppy felt adrift in the dark and silence, conscious only of the man sitting opposite her. He alone was real and solid. There was nothing but his face and his hands and his lean, hard body.

Her gaze skittered away from his mouth to the candle, and then back to his mouth, slid desperately along his jaw, before sneaking back to his mouth again. The memory of his kiss, that single, shattering kiss, was all at once so vivid that she could almost feel his lips against hers, could feel her body burn and throb where his hands had touched her.

Poppy swallowed. She must say something, do something.

'I'll get some coffee,' she gasped, pushing back her chair in desperation, and terribly afraid that she would simply dissolve in a puddle of desire at his feet if she didn't get to the kitchen in time.

She filled the kettle with shaking hands and went to stand outside on the back veranda while it boiled on the gas-ring. The night air was hot, as hot as the blood pounding insistently in her veins, but she wrapped her arms around herself as if she was chilled. How was she going to get through the evening without touching him?

'Good evening, madam.' The nightwatchman's disembodied voice startled her. She could see the tip of his spear gleaming in the hazy moonlight, and she wished him a good evening in return, glad to have been diverted from the treacherous train of her thoughts.

Taking a few deep breaths, Poppy went back inside and carried the coffee through to the other room, proud of her steady hands and her steady smile. Keir had snuffed out the candles and lit instead a stubby gas-lamp which hissed gently in its white, surreal glow.

'The light's not good enough to read, I'm afraid. Why don't we have a game of Scrabble to pass the time?'

His voice was matter-of-fact, and Poppy seized on the idea to keep her mind occupied, but it made no difference. The board was laid on one corner of the low square bamboo coffee-table, and they sat close together—though careful not to touch— so that they could both reach. Poppy soon slid off her chair to the floor, her long legs curled up beneath her and head bent over her tiles. Keir hunched forward on his chair, his elbows resting on his knees, hands steepled to his chin. Poppy was agonisingly aware of his knee only inches from her head, and his hand, lit up by the spluttering light of the lamp as he put down his tiles.

It was impossible to concentrate. She stared at the letters in front of her and could only think of words like 'kiss' or 'touch' or 'stroke'. She couldn't think of anything except Keir and how much she wanted him to touch her.

Everything seemed to be happening in slow motion; the languid movement of her fingers against the tiles, Keir's scratching his cheek thoughtfully, even the frantic night-time clamour of the insects had subsided, leaving only the uneven thud of her heart loud in her ears. Surely Keir could hear it?

They played in a silence which became subtly charged with tension as the game wore on. Poppy kept her eyes fixed on the board; if she looked at Keir she was lost.

It was no good; she couldn't think of another word. When Keir moved restlessly, Poppy put down 'kiss' and then made a great performance of scrabbling in the tin for some more tiles.

'Nine points,' she said, but her mouth was so dry that it came out like a whisper.

The tension tightened another notch, and, although she refused to look at him, and gazed determinedly at her tiles, Poppy knew that Keir's eyes were on her.

There was a pause. She could hear the light clicks as Keir rearranged his letters. He leant forward with only two tiles, which he put down very deliberately, one on either side of an 'o'.

'You'.

'Shall I?' he said softly.

Slowly, very slowly, Poppy raised her head. Keir was watching the way the sudden flare and hiss of the gas-lamp illuminated the pure line of her throat. The wayward curls had been pushed impatiently behind her ears as she pondered over the game, and her huge eyes gleamed up at him through the shadows.

Almost reluctantly, he reached down to stroke her soft cheek with one finger, a light tantalising caress, but enough to kindle the insistent glow of desire into a flame. When his hand cupped her chin to pull her up between his knees, she went unresistingly.

'Shall I?' he asked again, his voice deep and low and barely more than a whisper.

'Shall you what?' Poppy was beyond thinking. She was mesmerised by his eyes, which were alight with a warmth she had never seen there before, and giddy with the rush of sensation aroused by his touch.

'Shall I kiss you?' Keir held her face between his hands, tangling his fingers in her hair.

Instinctively Poppy rested her hands on his thighs for balance as she knelt before him. The muscles of his leg were tense beneath her fingers, and his hands were warm and strong against her face. Her body tingled, ached for him as she stared up into his face with eyes that shone, reflecting the lamplight and the longing in her heart.

'Yes,' she breathed.

Keir was smiling as he bent his head. 'Yes what?' he teased, but his voice was ragged as he traced the contours of her face with a thumb. His other hand slid under her curls to find the soft, sensitive hollow below her ear.

She could feel him smiling against her skin as he kissed it, and quivered with anticipation. 'Yes, please!' she gasped, her fingers tightening against his legs. 'Please kiss me!'

Keir lifted his head very slightly to look down into her face, his mouth twisted in a smile that was both rueful and tender, and then at last—at last!—his lips met hers.

Poppy closed her eyes and let exquisite release swamp her as she sank into his kiss. His mouth was warm, persuasive, unravelling her last defence, and she surrendered herself to the whirling delight of his taste and his touch, giving back kiss for kiss as desire, unfettered, coiled around them, binding them closer and closer with deepening need.

Both were gasping for breath when Keir broke off to pull her on to his lap. His arms tightened around her, his hands hard and urgent against her body, and Poppy gasped with inarticulate pleasure.

'Poppy!' Keir buried his face in her neck, breathing in her fragrance. 'You're so soft, so warm. I can't concentrate on anything except you...' His lips traced a burning path back to her mouth. 'I knew you'd be trouble, the first time I saw you!'

'I'm sorry...' Poppy was hardly aware of what she was saying. Her hands slid over him. She was desperate with the joy of being able to touch him at last, as she pressed kisses feverishly to his hair, his ear, his temple, arching her own throat to his devastating exploration.

They were tangled in a fiery web of passion which caught them tighter with every touch, burning higher and higher until Keir lifted her in his arms, and carried her to bed.

Poppy fumbled with the buttons on his shirt while he peeled off her clothes and let his hands drift over her skin in sensuous discovery. Her body responded instinctively to the insistence of his touch and she gasped his name, afire with need. He was hard beneath her touch as her fingers spread against the sleek strength of his back.

'I've been thinking about this ever since you arrived,' Keir mumbled into her hair. His hands slid lower, the need more urgent now, and his mouth followed to linger in the secret dips and curves of her body, leaving Poppy shuddering with abandoned delight.

'Coo—ee! Keir!' Astrid's voice ripped through the enchantment like a knife. 'Is anybody there?'

It was as if someone had thrown a bucket of cold water over them. For an endless moment Keir lay like a stone, one hand at her breast, mouth pressed to the hollow at the base of her throat, and then he disentangled himself from Poppy and stood up. It was impossible to read his expression in the darkness as he tucked his shirt into his trousers. He touched her hair very briefly. 'Stay here,' he mouthed.

'There you are!' Astrid's voice was sharp as Keir appeared. 'I thought for an awful moment you'd forgotten!'

'Forgotten?' Keir sounded distant.

'We promised we'd go and see the chief of police this evening. I told you about it this morning! The governor's assistant is staying with him and you agreed that it was essential that we go and talk to him before he goes back tomorrow. How could you have forgotten?'

'I've had other things on my mind,' Keir said slowly.

Astrid sniffed. 'Like that awful girl, I suppose! I can see why she would be distracting!' Suspicion crept into her voice. 'Where is she, anyway? And why is it all dark?'

'The generator broke down. And Poppy's . . . in bed.'

'In bed! At this time? It's only half-past eight!' Poppy could hear Astrid's heels clicking across the floor. 'That girl's just lazy, if you ask me!'

'It feels later when there's no light.' Keir hesitated. 'I was just about to go to bed myself.'

'It's lucky I came round when I did, isn't it?'

Poppy rolled herself into a ball and clenched her fists against her head at Astrid's self-satisfied tone. Lucky! Poppy's body throbbed with frustration and her breathing was still deep and uneven.

'You *are* coming, aren't you, Keir?' Astrid asked as the silence lengthened. 'You said this man had the governor's ear, and that we had to talk to him to make sure they don't change their minds at the last moment.'

'Yes, I did,' Keir acknowledged heavily. 'And, yes, I should talk to him, I suppose.' There was a pause. 'Just let me get changed.'

Poppy could hear him moving about in the other room as he changed his shirt. She lay, still tightly curled up, and imagined Astrid looking smug, drumming her immaculate fingernails impatiently on the veranda rail.

The door opened, and Keir came in, closing it softly behind him. Poppy looked at the wall; she couldn't bear to look at him.

'It's all right,' she said flatly. 'I heard.'

'I'm sorry,' he said in a even voice. 'But the project——'

'Is more important. I know.' She knew she sounded petulant, but she ached with unsatisfied need and all she could think of was that Keir had chosen to go with Astrid instead of staying with her.

CHAPTER EIGHT

POPPY lay rigid long after they had gone. She had been so sure that Keir wanted her as much as she wanted him. He had kissed her as if he loved her—but if he loved her, he would hardly have left her as he had done. She thought about his kisses, about the sweet intimacy of his touch and the surging delight.

Poppy turned on her stomach and punched her pillow into submission. It was impossible to believe that Keir had simply been passing a long, dark evening. He wasn't the type. He would do what he had to, and then make his excuses as soon as he could. Poppy closed her eyes and imagined Keir hurrying back to her. She imagined the quiet click of the door, the sound of his footsteps coming over to the bed, and then she would roll over and smile up at him, would reach up to pull him back into her arms... The thought warmed her, and she smiled into the darkness, remembering.

But Keir did not hurry back.

Poppy waited until the realisation that he was not coming drained the warmth from her, leaving her cold and empty. Knowing that she was here, loving and eager, he was lingering with Astrid, sharing the dark, warm intimacy of a tropical night with her. Was he confessing, admitting that Astrid had arrived just in time to stop him making a complete fool of himself? Or were they wondering what to do about the embarrassing way Poppy had thrown herself at him and begged him to make love to her? Or, worse, had he forgotten her entirely, put her out of his mind as soon as Astrid had taken his arm?

Poppy lay in stony-eyed misery as the possibilities circled through her mind. Frustration gave way to anger, and anger to bitter humiliation. It didn't matter what Keir was doing; what mattered was that he obviously didn't want to make love to her any more.

She strained to hear the sound of Keir's return, the sound that would mean he had come back to her after all, but the jungle noises reverberated undisturbed and at last Poppy lost her battle against tears as she cried herself to lonely sleep.

Poppy sat on a fallen tree and contemplated somewhat uneasily the long, thin column of soldier ants streaming across the path in front of her. She had never seen so many ants before! They marched in well-ordered formation, their sense of purpose as intimidating as their fearsome size.

Intrigued by their unwavering progress, Poppy leant forward to watch them more closely. If only life were that simple, she thought. You had no heartache if you were an ant, no hopeless longing, no jealousy, no humiliating tears or sleepless nights.

She wished she were an ant.

Her meeting with Keir that morning had been brief and uncomfortable. Poppy, terrified that she would betray how desperately hurt she was, had

retreated behind a mask of cool unconcern while
Keir, after one look at her face, had been brusque.
Neither had referred to the night before, although
the memory burned between them.

'I'm going to be working on the report with
Astrid today,' he said abruptly. 'We can't afford to
waste any more time.'

Wasting time? Is that what last night had been
for him?

'Fine,' said Poppy lightly. 'I thought I'd walk
out towards that village we passed the other day in
the forest. I could get some good photos.'

'Fine.'

'Fine.'

Their eyes slid away from each other.

Astrid had arrived just then, and Poppy had set
off soon after, unable to bear to see them together.
She walked the first couple of miles in a mood of
tremulous misery, until gradually pride came to her
rescue and her chin lifted. It wasn't all her fault!
Keir had no right to make love to her and then
ignore her. He had kissed her first, after all, and
she *hadn't* flung herself at him!

Her step became brisker. It was easier to be angry
than to be hurt. She was sick of being treated as a
nuisance. She was sick of being patronised by
Astrid, sick of being lectured about their wretched
project. She would leave here in a few days and fly
home and never see them again, and she would be
glad!

Liar, said her heart.

When the path forked, she took the left-hand
path which led into the forest. The trails between

the villages were easy to follow and she had little fear of getting lost here. This was a well-trodden path, and every now and then she passed clearings where someone had planted yams or a couple of banana trees.

It was quiet in the forest, and her sense of proportion was slowly restored by the hot stillness of the tangled growth. It was like walking through a giant conservatory, with plants Poppy was more used to seeing in tidy pots growing rampant— palms, ferns and enormous clumps of bamboo as big as a house. Occasionally she met a hunter with a dead monkey slung over his shoulder, or a farmer, machete in hand, returning from his plot, or children running barefoot along the dusty path, and she would exchange cheery greetings with all, but for the most part she was alone in the lush, green silence.

By the time she reached the fallen tree Poppy was hot and glad to stop for a drink. She sank on to the tree, thinking about the times she had stopped with Keir, and realising, with something of a shock, how much she was missing him. His image was so vivid that she half expected him to materialise beside her. She could picture the way he tilted his head to identify some jungle sound, the way he bent to retie his boots, the way he looked at her with that lurking, half exasperated smile.

Poppy's heart twisted with a longing so sharp that she almost gasped aloud. She had deliberately tried not to think about last night, but now she was submerged in a tide of bittersweet memories, the sweetness of shared delight and the bitterness of knowing the delight had not been shared at all. It had all been on her side.

She moved restlessly, as if she could feel his hands against her skin still, his lips against hers. She must try and put it out of her mind, as Keir so clearly had. She glanced around, desperate to distract her mind, and it was then that she saw the ants streaming across the path close to her feet.

Automatically, she reached for her camera. A cluster of ants struggled in unison to carry a leaf many times bigger than they were. Their air of concentration and team effort would make a great photograph for Thorpe Halliwell, she realised.

Changing the lens on her camera with the speed born of long experience, she tried to focus on the little group, but the angle was all wrong from where she sat. With some reluctance she lay on her stomach on the path, keeping a respectful distance from the ants. She had heard they could give a nasty bite. Fortunately, she had a good zoom lens and the ants marched stolidly onwards, unaware that they were being recorded for posterity.

Absorbed in what she was doing, she didn't hear anyone approach until a voice from above her spoke with some amusement.

'Well, hello, there! It's Poppy, isn't it?'

Poppy glanced up, startled, and then scrambled to her feet. It was Ryan Saunders.

'Er—hello.' She eyed him dubiously. All those involved with the project talked of him as if he was an arch-fiend, an evil schemer capable of single-handedly destroying the rain forest, but here in the dappled jungle light he looked perfectly normal.

'I suppose by now you've heard what a thoroughly bad lot I am,' he said, as if reading her mind, the boyish charm much in evidence, and when Poppy looked uncertain he laughed. 'Don't worry, I know what Keir Traherne thinks of me—he's never backward in letting you know exactly how he feels, is he?'

Poppy thought about last night. 'Oh, I don't know about that,' she murmured, almost to herself. Things would have been easier all along if she had known exactly how Keir felt!

Ryan didn't seem to notice her interruption. 'Actually, that's why I didn't come round and see you right away. I knew Keir would boot me out without letting me explain—as usual!—and I thought it might make things a bit awkward for you. Did you tell him we'd met?'

'No,' said Poppy slowly. 'No, I didn't.' Something in Ryan's manner made her uncomfortable, as if they were conspirators together. She hadn't mentioned Ryan, initially because there had never seemed to be the right time, and later because she had quite simply forgotten about him.

'Good.' Ryan stuck his hands in his pockets and looked at Poppy. She looked grubby, but oddly appealing, with her tousled curls and enormous, unhappy eyes. 'I was rather hoping I'd bump into you alone,' he went on, with a practised smile.

'Why?' Poppy asked bluntly.

'Why does any man want to bump into a pretty girl like you?' he countered, but at the look in Poppy's eyes, he stopped and shrugged. 'All right, I admit it. I want a chance to put my point of view to Keir, and I thought you might be a good way into the "other camp". The fact is that we've reached a stalemate in Adouaba. I can see that, even if Keir won't accept it. I need to talk to him, see if we can't work out some sort of compromise, but he refuses to even listen to me.'

'He's hardly likely to listen to me, either,' Poppy said with a touch of bitterness. She had turned away and was returning the zoom lens to its case.

'I heard you'd been sent out here by one of the project's major sponsors. He could hardly throw you out on your ear just for having a different opinion.'

'Perhaps my opinion is the same as Keir's.' She looked at Ryan with direct green eyes.

'I can't believe you're that narrow-minded,' said Ryan, meeting her gaze guilelessly.

'What do you mean?'

'You've heard the project's point of view. Fair enough. But you can't have an opinion without hearing my proposal.' He held up a hand when she would have spoken. 'Oh, you may have heard what Keir Traherne has told you, but he is, to say the very least, rather biased. He doesn't really know what our proposals are. My guess is that you're more open-minded than the great Dr Traherne and that you're not the kind of girl who'd let him or his iceberg of a girlfriend make up her mind for her.'

Poppy only really heard the last part of this speech. 'His girlfriend?' she repeated dully.

'You know, that frosty looking female...Anna?'

'Astrid.' Her voice was tight and hard.

'That's it, Astrid. Always looking down her nose at you. I've always thought she and Keir Traherne were well suited—no need of a fridge when either of them is around.'

Poppy was concentrating on packing her camera away into her daypack. She hadn't expected the truth, spoken so casually, to hurt so much. It wasn't as if she hadn't suspected it, but there had always been the hope that Astrid was, after all, simply a colleague to keep her going. Now her self-delusion hit her like a slap in the face. Ryan had been in Adouaba some time, and had no reason to lie. He spoke of Keir and Astrid as if their relationship was an established fact.

Why had she closed her eyes to it? Astrid was everything Keir could desire. She was beautiful, intelligent, capable—an asset, and not the liability he considered Poppy to be. Last night, he had been carried away, only to be caught almost red-handed by his girlfriend. No wonder he had been embarrassed this morning! Poppy yanked the final strap into place with a savage tug.

'Look, Poppy,' Ryan said persuasively as she straightened, her eyes very clear and green. 'Why don't you come with me to Mokake now? It's one of the villages involved in our development plan and you could see for yourself what our proposal's about. You might still agree with Keir, but you might just realise that I'm not as bad as I'm painted instead. I'm willing to take the risk of your making up your own mind if you are!'

She hesitated. She didn't entirely trust Ryan Saunders, but neither did she want to go back to

Keir and Astrid. She would only be in the way. They'd be sitting there, heads together over their precious report . . . or would they have seized the chance of her being out to slip back to Astrid's house to make love? Poppy's fingers curled at the thought and she made up her mind suddenly.

'All right, I'll come.'

Ryan kept up a stream of glib chatter as they walked on towards the village, and Poppy couldn't help comparing it with Keir's quiet, confident progress. Keir looked at home in the forest in a way Ryan never would. The younger man had all the right clothes, but they were all just that bit too new.

His talk was all of cities too, of money-making deals and tube strikes. Ryan never looked around him; he walked along the forest path as if it were the platform at Waterloo.

In spite of her jealousy, Poppy missed Keir with a physical ache. Whatever he said about making up her own mind, Ryan seemed to have taken her agreement to accompany him as a defection to his side. If it hadn't been for the thought of Keir and Astrid, she would have turned back. It felt all wrong to be here with Ryan . . . and yet, what harm was there? He might have a point. Poppy knew to her cost how intolerant Keir could be. What if a compromise *was* possible? She could be doing Keir a favour by finding out exactly what the situation was.

Keir doesn't want any favours from you, she reminded herself bleakly, and trudged on behind Ryan.

At Mokake the path widened into a dusty clearing between a cluster of windowless wooden huts. The village seemed deserted, apart from a hen pecking listlessly in a doorway, and a dog sprawled in the shade of a tree. Once out from the shelter of the dim jungle, the midday heat was crushing, and Poppy felt limp and tired. She wished she hadn't come.

Ryan made his way to one of the huts. In response to his call, a young man appeared from the dark interior.

'This is Emmanuel,' Ryan explained. 'He translates for me with the chief.'

Emmanuel raised a laconic hand in greeting and led them to the largest hut in the village. This was evidently the chief's house, and Poppy hesitated in the doorway while her eyes adjusted to the change in light.

Half the village seemed to have materialised out of nowhere, and the room was suffocating. Somebody dragged up a stool for her to sit on while Ryan launched into a speech that was obviously well-rehearsed.

Poppy watched him dispassionately while he talked grandly about putting in a road, and creating jobs, and clearing 'just a small area' of the forest. He was very attractive, and it all sounded plausible; she wondered why she didn't believe a word of it.

The chief sat and listened, expressionless, but once Poppy caught him watching her with shrewd dark eyes and she flushed, certain that he knew she was part of the rival scientific project. He would think she was disloyal, or, worse, that she had had her head turned by Ryan's handsome face. She stared back at the chief with troubled green eyes, suddenly desperate for him to understand the mixture of hurt pride and naïveté that had brought her here.

Poppy was so sure that his perceptive gaze would somehow read her mind that she felt sick disappointment when he only smiled and turned back to Emmanuel.

Ryan was delighted with her. 'I knew it was a good idea to take you along,' he said as they set off back along the path some time later. 'That old chief only ever looks blank when I talk to him, but I could see he was taken with you. He's obviously got an eye for a pretty girl! Now that he sees you're on our side, he might come round to our point of view.'

Poppy stopped short. 'What do you mean, *on your side*?'

'Oh, just a figure of speech...' Ryan glanced at her warily, as if unsure of how to deal with the unexpectedly stern figure beside him. 'I shouldn't be talking about sides, you're right,' he said, evidently deciding to lay on the charm. 'After all, we all want what's best for Mokake. I'm just glad you came with me and listened to what I had to say.'

Poppy avoided his eyes. Ryan seemed to be able to turn on the warmly sincere act at will, and she was beginning to mistrust it.

'So,' Ryan persevered. 'What do you think? Surely you must agree that wanting to invest in a village like Mokake isn't all bad!'

'No,' she said cautiously. 'It's true, I couldn't really argue with anything you said about providing jobs and so on, but I didn't get the impression that the village was all that keen on the idea.'

'Oh, they'll come round to it when they see what's in it for them.' The glimpse of Ryan's cynicism through the charm set Poppy's teeth on edge, and she began to walk faster. 'I don't know why people like the high and mighty Dr Traherne are so suspicious,' he went on. 'Anyone would think I was some kind of conman!' He laughed confidently. 'I mean, do I look like a conman?'

Poppy looked at him, at the handsome features, the engaging grin, the sincere expression.

'No, you don't,' she said frankly. 'But then, the best conmen never do, do they?'

Ryan chose to take this as a joke, and laughed, but, even so, it was a long walk back to Adouaba. Ryan, who had evidently expected to convert Poppy to his cause much more easily, was silent, almost sulky, but she was absorbed in her own thoughts and barely noticed. She *had* almost fallen for Ryan's easy charm. It wasn't easy for her to fault his arguments, either. There was only the hint of calculation in his eyes to make her uneasy.

She trudged on, uncomfortably aware of her recently healed feet. It was later than she had thought. Would Keir look for her—or would he be too taken up with Astrid to notice that she wasn't there? Poppy longed to see him, but dreaded it at the same time. Last night's kisses burned at the edge of her mind: the more she tried to push away the memory, the more insistent it glowed.

She didn't think she could bear to go back to how they had been before, not after the way they had touched. It would be easier to go than to have to listen to stilted, embarrassed apologies and explanations, or to have to smile and agree that they were both sensible people, of course it didn't matter, naturally it would be better to pretend it never happened.

Poppy was so busy imagining this speech of Keir's, and what she would say in reply, that she didn't at first notice that it had started to rain, but by the time they reached the fork in the path leading back to Adouaba she was drenched. She hadn't intended to go so far when she had left that morning and had never thought about taking a waterproof. Ryan obviously had, but equally obviously didn't intend to offer it to her.

Why should he? Poppy thought drearily, turning up the collar of her shirt in a futile attempt to keep the rain from streaming off her hair down her neck. At least her camera was in a waterproof bag: it was the only thing she could think of to feel cheerful about.

The jungle, so soothing in the dappled sunlight that morning, had become dark and hostile. In her haste not to lose sight of Ryan, who was walking quickly ahead of her, Poppy slipped and stumbled along the wet path. She no longer worried about what Keir would say to her; all she wanted was to be safe and dry.

Ryan had stopped and was waiting for her just beyond the fork. 'I've got a vehicle at the end of the track, but I don't suppose you'll want me to drive you back to Keir's place, will you? Not very tactful.'

'I suppose not.' Poppy leant against a tree and tried to get her breath back.

'So you won't mind if I don't wait?'

Poppy closed her eyes. 'No, I don't mind,' she said defeatedly.

'You're a great girl,' Ryan said, obviously relieved. 'Well...I'll get along then. I'll be in touch!' He turned and hurried down the path before Poppy could tell him not to bother.

'Great!' Poppy muttered, watching his rapidly retreating back in disgust. With a sigh, she lifted her face to the rain. She was so wet that she couldn't get any wetter, and the stinging force of the drops was almost exhilarating. The noise was tremendous as water crashed down from the rumbling clouds on to countless thousands of leaves before splattering on the forest floor.

Light-headed with exhaustion and hunger, Poppy abandoned herself to the elements, letting the rain stream through her curls and down her throat, washing away some of the misery in the sheer enjoyment of sensation.

'Penelope!'

Poppy didn't hear Keir's furious voice until he was standing right in front of her, and she jerked upright, startled out of her trance, unable to comprehend how he had suddenly appeared, and overwhelmed by such a rush of joy at the sight of him that for a moment she felt as if her heart had stopped.

He looked angrier than she had ever seen him before. As sodden as she was, his hair was slicked to his head and, beneath dark brows drawn ferociously together, his light eyes blazed with intense rage and something that Poppy might have thought was relief if she had not known better. The lines of his face were tight with anger, his body rigid, and he exuded such emotion that the jungle seemed to shrink back around them.

Poppy blinked the rain out of her eyes. Her eyelashes were spiky with the wet, her curls hanging in dejected rats' tails. She knew Keir was livid with her, she knew that she ought to be miserable, but just to look at him was enough to set a smile growing within her. He was there and she was safe.

Wiping the wetness from her cheeks, she tried to think of something dignified to say, but it was impossible to resist the pressure within her.

She smiled.

For one awkward moment she thought Keir might explode. 'You think it's funny, do you, Penelope? I suppose it is a bit of a joke—me spending all day worrying about your being out on your own, while all the time you were with Ryan Saunders! Oh, don't try and deny it! Astrid saw him heading off after you, and I've just seen him scurrying down the path. I suppose you were going to pretend you'd never been together? Was the that idea?'

'Yes...no...I mean, I have been with him today, but it wasn't prearranged. I met him by accident.'

Poppy's smile, the first rush of happiness, was fading.

'Oh, really? How convenient!' They were having to shout at each other above the noise of the rain. 'Funny how you were so keen to be on your own today!'

Poppy's eyes were huge and green in her white face. 'Well, it was pretty obvious I wasn't welcome where you were!' she yelled back. 'I didn't exactly fancy a day playing gooseberry to you and Astrid, so I went for a walk, like I told you. Ryan happened to be going the same way, that's all.'

'I see. And did this just *happen* to be the first time you'd met?' Keir's eyes were still bright and cold with anger.

Poppy hesitated. 'No,' she admitted at last. 'I met him in Mbuka, on the way up here.'

'So you've known him all the time!' Keir dashed the rain from his face. 'Good grief, you've made a fool out of me, haven't you? I was quite taken in by those big, innocent eyes of yours. All the time I was telling you about our work, you must have been sniggering, waiting for the chance to tell Ryan Saunders all about it!'

'No! It wasn't like that! I only met him for a couple of minutes in Mbuka. I didn't know who he was!'

'Why didn't you tell me about it?'

'I don't know.' Poppy shrugged helplessly. 'There just never seemed to be the right moment. You were always cross with me for some reason or other, and I suppose I thought it would just make it worse if

I told you about him then. Anyway, I didn't think it mattered all that much.'

Keir looked at her incredulously. 'Didn't matter! That man has put the whole future of the project in jeopardy, and you don't think it matters?'

'It *doesn't* matter!' Poppy was warmed by surging temper. 'You and Astrid go on and on and on about your bloody project! You're obsessed by it! What difference does it make that I met him? I couldn't tell you because I knew you'd react exactly like this, as if I'm some kind of traitor for talking to someone who doesn't agree with you.' Her sense of unease with Ryan was forgotten in the heat of the argument. 'Ryan Saunders is entitled to his opinion. At least he's broadminded enough to try and come to some sort of compromise with you. You won't even listen to him!'

'Well, he seems to have won you over easily enough! Let me see, Ryan's going to turn all the villages into thriving communities? Bring in jobs? Cars? Everyone's going to be rich? Is that what he told you?'

Poppy nodded defiantly as she glared back at Keir. She brushed away the water dripping from her nose with the back of her hand.

'And you believed him?' Keir's voice was hoarse with shouting over the rain. 'Ryan Saunders doesn't give a damn about the quality of life in these villages. As soon as he's got a licence, he's going to move everybody out, so that he can clear the forest more efficiently, and make more money. If you think anything else, you're a fool!'

'You're going to think I'm a fool, whatever I do, aren't you?' Poppy challenged him, eyes snapping with anger.

'There have been occasions when I thought there might have been some hope for you, but you seem to persist in acting like a complete idiot!' Keir retorted.

'What's idiotic about being prepared to listen to somebody else's point of view? What's idiotic about going for a walk in the forest? That's all I've done today!'

'I suppose you didn't think that I might wonder where you were? You left before ten this morning, and it's now——' he glanced at his watch, shook the drops off it irritably '—seventeen minutes past five!'

'So what? Why should you worry?'

'Is there no limit to your thoughtlessness? You went out without food, without a waterproof, without a torch, without any safety equipment. You might have been lying out here with a broken ankle, or a snake bite. You might have been lost. Of course I worried!'

Poppy was shaking with a combination of cold and fury. 'You do surprise me! When I left this morning I had the impression you'd have been glad if you never set eyes on me again!'

'The feeling seemed to be mutual!'

'What?' Poppy was rocked off balance by his bitter comment.

'You made it very clear that you didn't want to discuss what happened last night. I assumed you wanted to forget it.'

'Oh, did you?' she shouted back. 'A pretty convenient assumption after you'd spent the night with another woman!'

Keir stopped and stared at her. They were both drenched, both hoarse, both glaring through the rain at each other. Keir was for once not looking his neat, crisp self. His eyes were screwed up against the rivulets of water, and his sodden clothes were splattered with mud.

'Is that what you think?' he asked slowly.

Poppy was in no better state. She was gasping at the unrelenting onslaught of the rain, her shirt clinging to the curves of her body. For no reason, she suddenly felt as if she were naked. She swallowed.

'It's not what I think. It's what I know!'

'Penelope! You sound jealous!'

Keir took a step closer and Poppy stepped back, only to find herself against the tree.

'Well, I'm not!' she flung at him, in desperate defence. 'You were right first time. I just want to forget last night!'

CHAPTER NINE

'DO YOU?' Keir's voice was low, but he was so close that Poppy could hear him clearly.

'Yes!' she said, but she couldn't look at him. She could feel the heat of his body as she blinked away the rain. The water streamed off her face and ran down her throat and between her breasts. It seeped through her trousers and dribbled down her ankles, but it felt as though her entire body was warm and alive with a life and awareness of its own. 'Yes,' she said again, to convince herself.

'Liar,' said Keir. He put the flat of his hand against her right cheek and forced her head round to face him. His palm was the only contact between them; it was as if it burnt against her skin.

Poppy's eyes slid frantically away from Keir's. With a supreme effort, she lifted both her arms to pull his hand from her face, but he was far stronger than she, and his hand slid voluntarily down the side of her neck, glancing over her shoulder, and then lingering over the swell of her breast to her waist, and finally to rest in the small of her back. Irresistibly, he drew her body close to his.

'Do you really want to forget about last night?' he whispered into her ear. 'I can't forget about it, Poppy. Can you?'

Poppy's hands were on his arms, her fingers tightening instinctively against the pulsing heat of his skin beneath the sodden shirt.

'Yes,' she muttered, keeping her eyes fixed on the pulse that beat in the hollow of his throat.

Keir pushed the dripping hair from her face with his free hand and tilted her chin. '*Can* you?'

Slowly, Poppy shook her head and she looked deep into his eyes. 'No,' she admitted at last.

He smiled, his normally cool eyes alight with warmth. 'I didn't think so,' he said, and then the questions and accusations were over as he jerked her closer in a kiss that left them both breathless.

Gasping, clinging, they laughed shakily, unprepared for the flame of passion that had caught and burned so quickly out of control. Careless of the pelting rain, Keir pushed her back against the tree as they kissed again. Poppy's arms were around his back, her fingers insistent against him, glorying in the feel of his body, pressing hot and strong against hers. Buttons on wet cotton were too hard to deal with, so she pulled his shirt out of his trousers, and slipped her hands under the sodden material to explore his spine.

She could feel the vibrations in his chest as he mumbled something into her neck, but the rain made it impossible for her to hear as she arched against him, quivering with longing, and murmuring her own needs against his warm male skin.

There was no thought of resisting as they slithered to the ground together, touching each other with urgent hands and wild, desperate kisses.

The rain poured cool, unnoticed, down on them. Once Poppy tilted her head back and the dripping vegetation swam suddenly into focus, but then Keir's lips were at her breast, and she gave herself up once more to the reeling delight of his touch.

This time there was no going back, no one to interrupt. As kisses deepened and touch tightened, the jungle and the rain and the damp forest floor beneath them slid away, until there was only skin upon skin, touch upon touch, and at last, the shuddering, heart-stopping ecstasy of fulfilment.

Very gradually, Poppy became aware of the wetness on her face once more. Warm and heavy, Keir's relaxed body was pinning her to the ground. Opening her eyes, she could see a million glistening leaves, each one sharp and clear, as if she had never been able to focus properly before.

'Poppy,' Keir said into her hair, before pressing a warm, tender kiss below her ear. 'What have you done to me? Once I was a quiet, well-ordered man—and look at me now!'

'I am looking at you,' Poppy pointed out between kisses. 'You look wonderful to me!'

'Soaking wet and covered in mud? Is that any way to make love?' There was a laugh in his voice as he pulled her to her feet and began to fasten her shirt with aching tenderness.

Poppy leant into him, rested her face against the inviting hollow of his neck, and sighed with happiness as his arms closed around her. 'I thought it was the best way,' she said.

Keir stroked her hair. She could feel him smiling. 'The best is yet to come,' he promised. 'And it doesn't involve catching pneumonia—which is what will happen if we stay here any longer.' He held her away from him slightly. 'Come on, let's go home.'

Poppy's feet squelched horribly in her trainers as they made their way along the path to the outskirts of Adouaba, but she was oblivious to the relentless downpour. She was walking on air, filled with a boundless contentment that ignored the gloom and the rain and the discomfort, and knew only the feel of Keir's hand in hers.

To her surprise, Keir's Land Rover was parked on the muddy track where the path ended.

'How did you know where I was?' she thought to ask as Keir climbed in beside her, shutting out the wet if not the noise. The sound of drumming rain against the metal roof was deafening, and she had to shout again to make herself heard.

'Astrid said that she seen Saunders set off after you, and his vehicle was parked down the track a bit, so I knew you'd have to come back this way. I stayed away as long as I could, and then I came up here to wait. I saw Saunders scuttling back alone, and when there was no sign of you I got worried and set off to find you.' He laid his arm along the back of his seat and touched her wet curls very lightly. 'It was such a relief to see you. You looked like some kind of water nymph, just standing there with your head back and your eyes closed.' His voice changed. 'Why did Saunders leave you behind?'

'I think he just wanted to get out of the rain, and I was being too slow. He did say that he would have given me a lift, only he didn't think it would be a good idea for you to see us together.'

'It certainly wouldn't have been a good idea for him,' Keir said grimly, starting the engine and turning the Land Rover round. The wheels skidded in the mud a few times, and he drove cautiously until they hit the reassuringly firm tarmac.

'Isn't that Ryan's vehicle?' Poppy asked in surprise as they edged past a brand new jeep. 'I thought he'd have driven straight home.'

'He couldn't,' said Keir. He met her look blandly. 'I let all his tyres down. He obviously decided it was quicker to walk.'

Poppy was shivering by the time they reached the house. She stood in the bathroom and let the water puddle at her feet while Keir tested the shower.

'It's hot enough now,' he said and held out his hand. 'But there's only enough hot water for one shower. Come on!'

Without even bothering to strip off her clothes, she stepped under the stream of hot water with a rapturous sigh of relief.

'Better?' asked Keir, pulling her close so that they could share the heat.

'Much better.' Poppy slipped her arms round his neck. 'Much, much, much better!'

They clung together in the coiling steam, savouring the warmth and the stirring excitement as Keir peeled off her clothes and soaped her with leisurely strokes, his hands moving in sensuous circles until Poppy cried aloud with excitement.

Afterwards he dried her tenderly and carried her to bed and made love to her again. This time their

kisses were less desperate. They were warm and dry
and the anger that had fuelled their urgent passion
in the forest had been replaced by the glow of shared
delight. Now there was more time for uninhibited
exploration, for the thrill of discovering exactly
what touch could reduce the other to gasping, in-
coherent pleasure.

'Keir?' Poppy mumbled against his shoulder
much later.

'Mmm?' He ran his hand possessively over her
thigh.

'Where's Astrid tonight? Are you going to be
called away again?'

Keir grinned. 'I sincerely hope not! Fortunately,
I happen to know that she's having dinner with Guy
and a couple of the scientists who came back with
him from the camp. You could still go if you
wanted . . .'

'It's tempting.' Poppy pretended to consider. 'But
I think I'd better stay and keep my eye on you.'

His expression suddenly serious, Keir leant on
one elbow to look down into her face. 'I wasn't
with Astrid last night—or any night, come to that.
Will you believe me?'

'Yes,' she said simply. She lifted a hand to touch
the creases at the edges of his eyes very gently.
'Where were you?'

'The governor's assistant was on rollicking
form—it was ages until I could get away. By then
I thought you'd be asleep. I didn't want to go back
and talk business with Astrid, so I said I'd walk
home. I needed to think.' His smile was rather
twisted as he looked at her. 'I never intended to

kiss you last night, you know. It just . . . happened.
When I was walking back, I thought I must have
been mad. The project's at a crucial stage—I
couldn't afford the time to get involved with you.
And then you seemed pretty cool this morning, so
I thought the best thing would be to pretend that
it had never happened.'

He stroked her shoulder, let his hand linger on
the warm swell of her breast. 'If only it had been
that easy! I thought about you all day, and the more
I thought about you, the crosser I got that I couldn't
concentrate. I ended up blaming you—when I set
out to find you this afternoon, Poppy, making love
to you was the last thing on my mind!'

Poppy's hands were drifting down over his ribs
to his flat stomach. She was smiling. 'And now?'

'Now?' Keir rolled her beneath him. 'Now it's
the only thing on my mind!'

'There's good news and bad news,' Keir said as he
climbed the veranda steps the next morning.

'Oh?' Poppy stretched happily in the chair. He
had been down to see Astrid to discuss the project's
next moves, and she had waited, confident that
nothing could mar her contentment this morning.

'You remember that I told you that Guy brought
two scientists back with him? A lot of the plants
here have well-recognised medicinal qualities, and
they think they've found a particularly rare species,
which might just be used in treatments for some of
the nastier diseases around. If they're right, it could
clinch our case with the Minister.' He tapped the
report he held in his hand. 'These plants are po-

tentially very lucrative, but they can only grow in a protected rain forest environment.'

'So the Minister gets conservation and profit?' Poppy looked at him curiously. 'That's obviously the good news. What's the bad?'

'Astrid and I are going to Yaoundé today. We need to talk to various ministries to finalise details before presenting our report.' He hesitated. 'It's a long trip from here. We won't be back until tomorrow.'

Poppy tried hard to put a good face on it, and even mustered a brave smile as she waved him off, but it was impossible to ignore the creeping suspicion that it had been a relief for Keir to get away. She talked to herself sternly, telling herself that she had no reason to be jealous, but the image of Astrid, sitting upright and immaculate next to Keir as they drove off, stayed with her all day.

She believed Keir when he said that Astrid was no more than a colleague, but feminine intuition told her that Astrid's motives were far from businesslike. 'Come on, Poppy,' she chided herself. 'He was with you last night, not Astrid. What more do you want?'

Sighing, she turned back into the house. The truth was, she had wanted some kind of reassurance that last night had not just been a momentary lapse for Keir. He had kissed her goodbye quite unselfconsciously, but she had been aware that his thoughts were elsewhere. He had taken her to new heights of awareness, had made her feel things she had never felt before, but there had been no mention of love or the future, had there? What she wanted, she realised, was to know that Keir would be hers every night, and not just when Astrid wasn't around to interrupt.

The day dragged by, overcast and sticky. Poppy was writing up her scribbled slide notes without much enthusiasm when a step on the veranda made her look up with a smile, expecting Gabriel, or Guy.

Ryan Saunders stood in the doorway with an exaggerated expression of little-boy guilt. 'Can I come in?' he asked, taking her agreement for granted and looking around the room, as if taking a mental inventory. 'I saw Keir and his blonde sidekick driving out of town earlier, so I thought it would be safe to come round and see if you got home all right yesterday.'

'Why are you so frightened of Keir?' Poppy asked lightly, putting down her pen. 'You're bigger than he is.'

Ryan paused, eyes slightly narrowed. 'I wouldn't say I was frightened. Wary, perhaps. There's a dangerous quality about him, isn't there? He never does anything dramatic, but you always know the danger is there.' He laughed. 'Well, maybe I am just a coward, but I did want to see you again, and I don't want to meet up with Keir unless I can help it.'

'I thought you wanted to talk to him,' Poppy said.

He looked momentarily disconcerted. 'Well, yes . . . but not when I'm talking to you.'

'I see.' Poppy pushed her curls behind her ears and regarded him thoughtfully. He seemed to be assessing the room, calculating eyes flickering from

Keir's desk covered with reports to the Thorpe Halliwell computer and back to the papers again. Suddenly it seemed imperative to get rid of him. She stood up.

'It was nice of you to come round, Ryan. I got back without any problems, as you can see. What about you?'

His face hardened. 'Some kids had let all the air out of my tyres. I had to walk all the way!'

Poppy clicked her tongue sympathetically. 'Who would do a thing like that?' She hoped she wouldn't betray herself by smiling. 'Well, I won't keep you...'

'You seem very anxious to get rid of me!' The self-conscious charm in his voice had acquired a slight edge.

'I don't think there's any point in us talking any more.' She faced him squarely. 'I listened to what you had to say yesterday, and I'm afraid I still think that Keir's project is the right one for this area.'

'The government won't think so, I can tell you that!' Ryan had dropped his façade of boyish charm. 'If they get the choice between a few namby-pamby scientists and a development like ours which will bring in lots of money I don't think they'll have much trouble making up their minds.'

Poppy's green eyes sparkled angrily at his jeering tone. 'I don't think they'll find it hard to decide either—not when they know they can have money and conservation at the same time.'

Ryan stilled. 'What do you mean, money *and* conservation?'

'Nothing!' Poppy said quickly. She was already regretting having mentioned it at all. Why didn't he leave?

'Has Traherne got something up his sleeve?'

'That's none of your business!' she retorted, but in spite of herself her eyes flickered towards the report lying on Keir's desk.

Seeing her look, Ryan pushed past her and snatched it up, easily fending off her efforts to grab it back. 'What's he saying?' he demanded, flicking through the pages to find the conclusion.

'Give that back to me!' Poppy hissed in a furious whisper, terrified that someone would arrive and see her apparently letting Ryan read the precious report.

'Not till I've finished with it ... aha! this must be it!' Ryan scanned the pages, his brows drawn together in a frown, but when he had finished he dropped the report back on the desk with a contemptuous smile. 'Making money from natural medicines! He's got to be joking!'

'I don't think the Minister will think so!' Poppy retorted, provoked. 'Money isn't everything, in spite of what you think. We've already had a hint that the government will opt for conservation, and now there's a financial advantage as well. I wouldn't be too sure they'll come down on your side.'

'Bah! Traherne's just bluffing! It's a good try, but he doesn't fool me. He'd do anything to stop our development, even if it involves a few lies——'

'He's not lying!'

'Isn't he? Oh, I know you believe him—nobody could fake that transparently innocent air you have—but I wouldn't put it past Keir Traherne to use you to convince others.' He looked at her speculatively. Her face was bright with indignation, mingled doubt and anger in her eyes. 'You're a useful asset. Why do you think I took you to the old chief in Mokake? One look in those big, innocent eyes and it's obvious you couldn't be mixed up in anything underhand. Having you with me was like a guarantee of honesty. And don't tell me Keir wasn't thinking exactly the same thing when he took you to the chief here!'

Poppy was so angry that she could barely speak. 'I think you'd better go!'

'Don't worry, I'm going.' Ryan sauntered to the door, turning for one last shot. 'When you see your precious Dr Traherne, tell him I haven't given up yet!'

Poppy stared after him with a troubled expression. She had been a fool to blurt it out like that to Ryan. Why hadn't she just kept her mouth shut?

She nibbled anxiously at a fingernail. If only Ryan hadn't seen the report! There was a ruthlessness about him which she hadn't seen before, and it made her uneasy. And yet, she tried to reassure herself, what could he do with the information? He might be better prepared, but it wouldn't change the facts, would it? She picked up the report and clutched it to her protectively. As long as Keir had this, he would win his licence.

By the evening, Poppy's niggling feeling of guilt had settled into a conviction that not too much harm had been done. Ryan had been worried—his gibes about Keir being reduced to lying proved that!—but so much the better. He would have found out sooner or later anyway. She would tell Keir about it when he got back, and he would know what to do...

Pushing Ryan Saunders from her mind, Poppy gave herself up to thoughts of Keir. She let Gabriel go home early and sat on the veranda, feeling the doubts and uncertainties of the day dissolve in memories of the night before. Remembering the feel of his body, the light in his eyes when he had kissed her, she was sure that he loved her, and nothing else seemed to matter.

She barely noticed when the generator broke down again. Absorbed in her thoughts, she lit a couple of candles and watched the flames leap and flicker. Tomorrow, when Keir came back, she would tell him how much she loved him, and he would say he loved her too and beg her to stay and everything would be perfect.

It didn't work out that way.

Wrapped in dreams of the day to come, Poppy floated to bed early and fell almost immediately into a deep, dreamless sleep.

She awoke to bright light. Her first thought was that the generator must have come on again of its own accord, but then, as her mind focused with a jolt, the meaning of the fierce glow, the sinister noise and the unmistakable smell of fire jerked her upright in terrified realisation.

Struggling to disentangle herself from the mosquito net, she grabbed her camera bag instinctively and ran for the door. One glance at the wicked leaping blaze was enough to make her slam it shut immediately. There was no way she could get to the door that way—the whole living-room was alight.

Poppy ran to the window. The house was all on ground level, so it should be easy to get out. But she had forgotten the strong wire netting that covered all the windows to keep the mosquitoes out at night. She tore at it frantically with her hands, really frightened for the first time.

'Help!' she cried, even as she realised that there was nobody there to hear her. 'Fire!'

Her hands were torn, her voice hoarse, when, incredibly, she heard voices. 'Help!' she yelled again, glancing over her shoulder at the door where the flames flickered insidiously.

'Poppy!' She was too panic-stricken to feel any surprise when Ryan Saunders's face appeared on the other side of the wire.

'I can't get out,' she sobbed.

'Hang on! I'll be straight back.' He disappeared, returning almost immediately with a large pair of pliers and a saw. Within a couple of minutes he had torn back the netting enough for her to wriggle out.

'We'd better get back. These wooden houses go up like tinderboxes.' Dragging her to her feet, he pulled her to the safety of the track, where she collapsed, shaking with reaction and still clutching her camera bag.

There were shouts in the distance, then running feet. Poppy coughed and wiped her streaming eyes as people gathered round her, all talking and gesticulating wildly at the blazing house.

'Can't we do anything to stop it?' she croaked helplessly.

'I'm afraid not.' Guy had appeared from somewhere, and he helped her to her feet with a grim face. 'It's too late to save anything now.'

'But Keir's report . . . all his papers . . .'

'There won't be anything left of them now.' Sick at heart, they stood as if mesmerised by the flames and watched the house slowly collapse in on itself.

It was only later that Poppy realised that, after saving her, Ryan had quietly disappeared before the crowd arrived.

Keir stood and looked at the blackened remains of his house. His face was empty of all expression.

'How did it start?'

They all looked at Poppy. 'I don't know,' she said helplessly. 'I was asleep.'

'These things usually start from a cigarette or something,' Astrid observed. 'It was obviously something inside the house, anyway.'

'Perhaps a candle,' put in the chief of police, who was watching his men pick over the ruins with glum satisfaction.

Something cold closed over Poppy's heart. It must have shown in her face, for Astrid looked at her more closely. '*Did* you have a candle last night, Penelope?'

'The generator broke down . . . I only lit a couple.'

'It only takes one,' said Keir bitterly. 'Didn't you think to put them out—or was that too much trouble?'

'I think I did . . . I can't remember,' she cried desperately. 'It's all so unreal now! I just can't remember!'

He looked at her with eyes that were so cold that she thought her heart would break. 'You can't remember,' he repeated heavily. 'Do you realise what you've done? Do you know how many hours of work we've put into that report? All our records, all our papers, all gone! And all because of you! We've nothing to show the minister now—we might as well hand Ryan Saunders his licence right now!'

Ryan Saunders! An awful suspicion crept over her. 'Ryan was here last night,' Poppy said slowly, almost to herself.

Keir's eyes narrowed to slits of steel. 'Saunders? Here?' He glanced at Guy. 'Did you see him?'

Guy shifted uncomfortably. 'Well, no . . . when I got here there was just Poppy. She was in a bad way.'

'But he *was* here!' Poppy felt as if everything inside her had shrivelled to a hard knot of despair.

'I see. So it was all the invisible Ryan's fault. Nothing to do with Poppy being her usual careless self!' Keir's voice was icy with contempt. 'I thought you of all people wouldn't try and throw the blame on anyone else—even Ryan Saunders.' Taking her wrist in a savage grip, he pulled her to one side. 'You've gone too far this time, Penelope. All you were supposed to do was come out and take a few photographs. Was that so hard? Instead, you've been a nuisance, an embarrassment, a damned distraction when I most need to concentrate, and now you've destroyed three years' work with your criminal carelessness. Are you satisfied now?'

Poppy's eyes were enormous with anguish and the appalling, nagging doubt that she was, after all to blame. 'I'm sorry,' she whispered.

'You're sorry!' His face twisted with bitterness. 'Not as sorry as I am that I ever set eyes on you! You can go back to Thorpe Halliwell and tell them all the sponsorship in the world isn't worth the trouble you've caused us!'

CHAPTER TEN

ASTRID found Poppy on Guy's veranda. She was
sitting huddled up as if she were cold.

'Ah, there you are!' Astrid said briskly. She sat
down next to Poppy and flicked over a few sheets
on her clipboard. 'Keir's gone straight back to
Yaoundé to try and explain away this mess to the
Minister. I—we—think it would be a good idea if
you weren't here when he gets back.'

Poppy stared at her with stricken eyes. 'Did Keir
say that?'

'I mentioned it to him, and he—er—indicated
that he thought it was a good idea.' She paused
delicately. 'I won't distress you by repeating exactly
what he said.'

'And he's gone already? Without saying
goodbye?'

'He's got rather a lot on his mind just now,' said
Astrid pointedly. 'I'm not surprised he didn't feel
up to a fond farewell, are you?'

Poppy felt as if she would shatter at the slightest
word or movement. 'No,' she whispered.

'I know you're rather smitten with Keir,' said
Astrid, 'but look at it from his point of view. He's
been out here a long time on his own. Suddenly,
there's a girl only too willing to fall into his
arms... well, who can blame him for being distracted?' She smoothed her hair back com-

172

placently. 'I know what these men are like, Poppy.
Their work is their life. Of course they need a
woman occasionally, but in the long run women
are just a distraction for them. Keir doesn't need
any more distractions at the moment, and I think
it would be less embarrassing for him if you just
left him alone to salvage what he can of the project.'

Her sharp blue eyes inspected Poppy's averted
face. 'Quite apart from anything else, he's very
angry with you—understandably so. I know that
nothing's been proved, but the general feeling is
that it was your carelessness that started the fire
and destroyed any chance of the project's con-
tinuing. I'd have thought you'd want to go home.'

'Would you?' Poppy stood up and looked at
Astrid, woman to woman. Her eyes were a deep,
anguished green in her tired face, but now there
was a spark of anger in them. 'Can I ask you
something?'

Astrid was taken aback. 'Yes.'

'Haven't you ever wished that you were a distraction to Keir?'

Something flickered in Astrid's face. 'No. I consider myself to be Keir's colleague. My satisfaction
comes from the project,' she said pompously. 'I'm
not jealous because Keir found you attractive, I can
assure you. I know that he'll come back to me because the project is the most important thing for
both of us.'

Poppy stared at her. 'You don't know what
you're missing!'

'At least I'll still have Keir!' Astrid retorted, and
then caught herself up, horrified at the way her

poise had deserted her. Recovering herself, she went on, 'I never liked you! You threatened the project right from the start, taking up Keir's valuable time, creating quite the wrong impression, blundering around ... and look what it's led to! You've ruined everything!'

'Yes,' Poppy agreed quietly. 'I seem to have.'

'I'm glad you've got the decency to admit it! Now, do you want me to fix this flight for you or not?'

The silence lengthened as Poppy thought about never seeing Keir again, never having the chance to tell him how much she loved him. Then she thought about the contempt in his voice, about seeing the disgust in his eyes as he pushed her away. At last, reluctantly, she nodded.

With ruthless efficiency, Astrid altered her ticket and arranged for people travelling to Douala to give Poppy a lift to the airport. Later, Poppy could remember nothing of the journey. She checked in at the airport, moving jerkily like a robot, seeing things through a blur of misery.

She sat stiffly on the plastic seats in the departure lounge, her mind circling round an endless series of 'if onlys'... If only the generator hadn't broken down, if only Keir had not had to go to Yaoundé, if only he had believed her, if only she had had a chance to see him just once more...

Suddenly she stiffened. Across the room, Ryan Saunders was slipping his boarding-card into his jacket pocket, glancing indifferently about him. His gaze fell on Poppy, and for a moment he looked wary, before he evidently decided to brazen it out and strolled over.

'Hello, there.'

Poppy's eyes were stony. 'I didn't expect to see you here. I thought you'd be busy sucking up to the Minister.'

'Oh, I've done plenty of that. Now I'm going home to fix up some finance . . . I think we're going to be needing it.'

'You started that fire, didn't you, Ryan?' She stared at him with loathing.

Ryan smirked. 'It turned out to be quite a show, didn't it? It worked far better than I expected.'

'I might have died,' she whispered.

'I'd forgotten about that netting, I must admit. I just wanted to get rid of Keir's papers—I didn't want anyone to see me there. I wasn't bargaining on having to rescue you.'

'I'm surprised you bothered,' Poppy said bitterly.

He affected a hurt look. 'What do you think I am?'

'I think you're despicable!'

'Oh, don't be like that, Poppy. What's the matter? Didn't they believe that I was there? That's too bad! After all I had to say about your transparent innocence, too!'

'They think it was an accident—I don't think any of them could conceive of anyone's being coward enough to do something like that deliberately! You must have been really worried by those—what did you call them?—"namby-pamby scientists".'

His face hardened. 'I'm not worried by them any more,' he said with a cold, cruel smile. 'That's business, Poppy.'

'These photographs are absolutely superb!' Don Jones shook his head in admiration. 'My favourite is that one of the postbox—what a great picture!' He turned back to Poppy, who stood gazing out of the window at the jostling London crowds. 'They're just what we wanted, Poppy—well done!'

She mustered a smile. 'I'm glad you're pleased.'

'Pleased! The chairman's delighted! I suppose you've seen that the ads are out already? We did a special rush job.'

Poppy nodded. It seemed you couldn't pick up a magazine without seeing a glossy spread of the rain forest with the Thorpe Halliwell distinctive logo. There were huge enlargements in the Underground, and a series of smaller posters slid past inexorably as you were carried up the escalators. For Poppy it was bittersweet. Every picture brought a pang of memory: there was that butterfly she had taken so long to photograph, there was the scientists' camp, there was the magnificent tree straddling the path where they had stopped to rest.

She thought about Cameroon the whole time, about the forest and the people and the markets, but mostly about Keir. She missed him with a physical ache. She had tried to pick up the threads of her life, but struggled against an indifference that threatened to swamp her. While she was dutifully laughing at friends' jokes, or pretending an interest in the latest gossip, her thoughts would slide treacherously back to Africa.

Where was Keir? What was he doing? She imagined him leaning back on his chair, stretching wearily, or holding a mug of tea between his hands as he discussed some problem with the scientists. Perhaps he was frantically rewriting his report? She preferred to imagine him hunkering down by a fire out in the forest, surrounded by the sounds and smells of the night air. Sometimes Poppy would lie in bed and remember the pulsating, raucous atmosphere, and despair that the only sign of life she could hear now was the distant wail of a siren, or a car changing gear in the darkness.

Poppy had never known what real unhappiness was before. Worst of all was the guilt. Poppy had an innate honesty that forced her to recognise that although it hadn't been her carelessness that had started the fire she might have provoked Ryan into desperate measures. She had even let him see the report—she might as well have lit the candle herself! What a fool she had been! No wonder Keir had turned from her in disgust! She had deserved everything he had said to her.

'You're not your usual cheerful self, Poppy.' Don Jones was watching her with concern. 'Is everything OK?'

Poppy started to smile and say yes, of course, but to her horror her mouth started to tremble uncontrollably. Appalled, she covered it with her hand, but it was too late. The tears welled up and splashed on to her hand.

Don put a fatherly arm around her shoulders and urged her to a chair. 'I think you'd better tell me all about it.'

When she had gasped out the whole story between wracking sobs, Poppy screwed up the handkerchief he had handed her into a soggy ball and wiped her eyes with a juddering sigh. 'I just feel it's all my fault! If only I could do something to make up for it. I wondered...' She glanced at Don. 'I wondered if Thorpe Halliwell would sponsor them again—without wanting to send a photographer...' She trailed off.

Don looked up from twisting his coffee-cup thoughtfully in its saucer, and to her relief he smiled. 'I'll talk to the chairman about it,' he promised. 'In the meantime, I've a favour to ask you.'

'A favour?' Poppy echoed, surprised.

'My daughter's getting married at the end of the month. I wondered if you'd mind doing the photos?' He shrugged self-consciously. 'You're the best photographer I know and, well, Sue's my only daughter. I want the best for her.'

It was a lovely day for a wedding. High in the sky, billowing clouds scudded past on a brisk wind, but the air was bright and clear with the promise of spring. Outside the church, clusters of guests stood around, holding their hats against the breeze and watching as Poppy arranged everyone for the group photographs.

For Don's sake, she had made an effort and was wearing her best dress. Patterned with bold red flowers, the skirt swayed and swirled exuberantly as she walked. It was an eyecatching outfit that suited her tall, slim figure and vibrant personality and normally it made her feel good just to wear it, but today her smile was strained. It needed more than a dress to raise her spirits now.

At least the bride and groom looked radiantly happy, she thought as she regrouped the brides-maids, and Don Jones was bursting with pride, beaming and winking in the background. Perhaps it was time she made a real effort to pull herself together and get on with her life. Push Keir Traherne into a mental cupboard marked 'Out of Reach' and shut the door. She had learnt her lesson. From now on she would be a new person, smart, careful, on top of things.

'Poppy!' Don Jones was at her elbow again. 'I think it's time we all headed down to the reception and broke open the champagne. Have you got enough photos for now?'

She nodded, smiling. 'I think so.'

'In that case, I'll get everyone moving. You are coming to the reception, aren't you?'

'Of course.' A gust of wind blew her curls about and she pushed them away from her face. 'I just need to put all this equipment away, then I'll come along.'

She began packing away her cameras as Don shepherded the guests towards the reception. Her feet ached in unfamiliar high-heeled shoes, and she was about to kick them off when one of the narrow heels caught in between the paving stones so that she stumbled and fell.

Picking herself up, she rubbed her grazed knees and regarded her muddied, laddered tights with resignation. She had never mastered the art of wearing tights for a whole day without ruining them. So much for the smart new Poppy Sharp!

The offending shoe lay still wedged on the path, its heel wrenched sideways. Poppy tugged it free and limped over to an old gravestone to inspect the damage.

Now that the guests were gone, it was very quiet in the churchyard. It was good to have a few minutes to herself. The shoe forgotten in her hands, Poppy turned her face up to the sun and the wind, and, despite every firm resolution, allowed herself to think about Keir, the sound of his voice, the shape of his mouth, the touch of his hands.

'Poppy.'

Poppy heard her name with a sense of unreality. For a moment she didn't move, unwilling to open her eyes and see someone who wasn't Keir. It had sounded so like him that she felt tears prick her eyelids. She couldn't bear it not to be him!

'Poppy!' The voice held an undercurrent—of laughter? exasperation?—that could not be mistaken.

Very slowly, hardly daring to breathe, Poppy opened her eyes, wide and green and shimmering with unshed tears.

'Keir?' It was barely more than a whisper.

He was standing in front of her, in a rather shabby tweed jacket, his tie whipped by the wind. The startlingly light eyes looked tired, and there were lines of strain about his mouth.

Poppy could only stare and drink in the sight of him as the shoe fell unheeded from her hand. He looked wonderful.

'I didn't recognise you at first,' he said, almost awkwardly. 'Don Jones told me you'd be here. He said he didn't think you'd mind if he told me.' He hesitated. 'I've been watching you. You looked so smart and professional—I couldn't believe it was you.'

She glanced at him uncertainly, then down at her dress. 'I suppose you've never seen me in proper clothes before.' Was that her voice, high and stilted?

'No.' His smile twisted and he nodded down at the broken shoe in the grass. 'Same old Poppy, though. When you fell over, it was almost a relief. I thought that that lovely girl might just be my Poppy after all.' Taking both her hands, he pulled her to her feet, until she was balanced precariously on one shoe.

The light in his eyes made Poppy's heart race with a wild, surging hope. Still in a daze, she kicked off her remaining shoe so that she had to look up into his face. 'What are you doing here?' was all she could ask, hopelessly adrift in the glorious, unexpected joy of seeing him. Her fingers curled around his of their own accord.

'I came to apologise.'

'You? Apologise to me?' Poppy's eyes widened with astonishment. 'But why? I should be apologising to you! Oh, Keir!' she rushed on, unable to stop now she had started. 'I wanted so much to tell you how sorry I was!'

Keir turned her hands over in his and stroked her palms with his thumbs, very tenderly. 'It wasn't your fault. I know that now. One of Gabriel's many cousins saw Saunders slipping away. As soon as I heard that, I knew you must have been right.' He looked into her eyes. 'I can't tell you how many times I've wanted to take back all those things I said to you that day, Poppy.'

'But Keir, it was all my fault! If it hadn't been for me blurting it out, Ryan would never have known about the new report, and he wouldn't have felt he had to act so quickly. I ruined everything!'

His hold on her hands tightened. 'Not quite. When it became clear that we'd been the victim of some very dirty tricks indeed, the Minister looked a little more closely at Saunders's proposal, and he wasn't impressed.'

'He gave you the licence after all!'

'Yes—another five years.' Keir smiled. 'And a lot of it's thanks to you.'

'To me?' Poppy's disbelief was almost comical.

'Yes, you. The Mokake chief said you looked so troubled when you were with Ryan that he immediately distrusted him, and Nesoah—you remember your drinking partner in Adouaba?—said that any project that you were involved in had his vote. He didn't care which one it was. I gather his support is based on the fact that you "drink like a man"!'

A smile trembled on Poppy's mouth. 'So my hangover was worth it?'

'It was. And so was what you did for us here. Don Jones told me that you'd suggested Thorpe Halliwell sponsor us again. Thanks to your photos, they're more than willing to build and equip a new headquarters—and that's just for starters. So you see, I've got a lot to thank you for, and even more to apologise for.'

He paused. 'I should never have said those things to you, Poppy. When I came back and found that you'd gone...' Keir looked over her shoulder at the old church and for a moment his grey eyes were unseeing. 'I can't describe how I felt.'

'But Astrid told me you wanted me to go!'

'I did—for about five minutes. As soon as I'd gone, I wanted to rush back and tell you I didn't mean it, but the whole project depended on my persuading the Minister to give us more time. I *had* to go—can you understand that, Poppy?'

'Of course,' she said softly. 'I know how much the project means to you.'

'When I got back, I couldn't believe that you weren't there. And then Astrid told me you'd left on the same flight as Ryan Saunders! At first it helped to be angry, but when I calmed down I knew that you wouldn't have gone with him, not after the night we shared together.' He dropped one of her hands to push the wind-blown curls gently back from her face. 'You wouldn't have, would you?'

Poppy shook her head. She could feel the happiness fizzing through her veins like champagne bubbles. 'No,' she said simply.

'I missed you so much, Poppy. Life went back to normal. Everything was organised, I could work without being distracted. It was what I claimed I always wanted. But I couldn't enjoy it any more.

Every time I heard someone coming, I'd look up, hoping against hope that it would be you.

'It was only when you'd gone that I realised how much fun you made everything seem—even when I was trying to be cross with you, I was always on the verge of laughter. It was so quiet without you. Gabriel has been drooping around with a face like a wet Sunday, all the scientists wanted to know why you'd gone, and I'm sick of people in the market asking when you're coming back.' He looked down into her eyes, his own questioning. 'I said I would have to come and ask you.'

'When I'm going back?' Poppy breathed, hardly able to believe that this was happening. 'But Keir, I'm such a disaster! You'll have so much work to do—you don't want to be distracted!'

'No,' he said unexpectedly. 'I don't.' His smile was wry as he pulled her close. 'You've wrecked my house, stirred up my project, broken all my crockery and thrown my life into confusion. I don't want to live in chaos, I don't want to be distracted from my work.' There was such warmth in his face that Poppy ached with happiness. 'But I can't live without you either, Poppy. You're the last type of woman I ever imagined falling in love with. You're scatty, you're scruffy, you're absolutely maddening at times, but you're warm and funny and beautiful, and I love you very, very much.'

Poppy's eyes were like stars. 'Keir...' She leant into him as his arms closed tighter about her. 'Do you really love me? Say it again!'

'I love you.' Tired of words, he bent his head and kissed her, a long kiss, deep and rough and tender, that left Poppy feeling as if she was dissolving in bliss.

'Aren't going to tell me that you love me too?' he mumbled into her curls.

'You know I do.' She smiled into his neck and kissed the warm pulse below his ear, shivering with delight as his hands tightened against her in response. 'I loved you even when you were telling me what a nuisance I was.'

'You *were* a nuisance,' Keir pointed out. 'You were the last thing I needed, but when I met you at the airport I knew I was doomed! You were a walking disaster, but you had such beautiful eyes and a smile that was pure mischief. I fought it for a long time. Why do you think I spent so long staring at the computer? I was desperate to concentrate on anything that wasn't you, but it was hopeless. I was aware of you even when you were being good and quiet—not that that was very often!'

Poppy pulled away slightly, her eyes suddenly serious. 'Are you sure about me going back? Won't I just get in the way again?'

'I've decided to give you a proper job to keep you out of mischief.'

'Photography is a real job,' she said, trying hard to sound offended.

'Ah, yes, but this one will keep you under my eye. I need a new assistant.'

Poppy stared at him. 'What about Astrid?'

'Astrid has been offered an excellent job by an aid organisation in Kenya,' he said with a studiedly non-commital expression. 'I'm sure she'll be able to make much better use of her talents there.'

'Oh.' Poppy looked doubtful. 'Well, I hope you don't expect me to be as efficient as Astrid.'

Keir laughed out loud. 'I expect you to be nothing but trouble,' he said, pulling her hard against him once more. 'In fact, I foresee a lifetime of trouble ahead.'

'A lifetime?' Poppy leant her head against his chest and listened to the reassuring beat of his heart.

'As leader of the project, I'm afraid I'm going to have to insist that you marry me. I have the reputation of the project to think of!'

'Of course!' Her green eyes brimmed with laughter.

'What's this?' He tilted her face up to his. 'No arguing? No determination to go off and do precisely what I didn't want you to do?'

Poppy smiled and pulled his head down until their lips met in a kiss that held a lifetime of promise. 'Not this time,' she said.

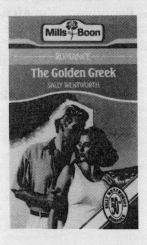

YOU <u>CAN</u> AFFORD THAT HOLIDAY

Great savings can be made when you book your next holiday – whether you wa to go skiing, take a luxury cruise, or lie in the Mediterranean sun – the Holiday Club offers you the chance to receive **FREE HOLIDAY SPENDING MONEY** wor up to 10% of the cost of your holiday!

All you have to do is choose a holiday from one of the major holiday companies including Thomson, Cosmos, Horizon, Cunard, Kuoni, Jetsave and many more

Just call us* and ask if the holiday company you wish to book with is included

HOW MUCH SPENDING MONEY WILL I RECEIVE?

The amount you receive is based on the basic price of your holiday. Add up the total cost for all holiday-makers listed on your booking form – excluding surcharges, supplements, insurance, car hire or special excursions where these are not included in the basic cost, and after any special reductions which may offered on the holiday – then compare the total with the price bands below:-

YOUR TOTAL BASIC HOLIDAY PRICE FOR ALL PASSENGERS	HOLIDAY SPENDING MONEY
£ 200 449	£ 20
450 649	30
650 849	40
850 1099	60
1100 1499	80
1500 1999	100 ...
... 8500 or more	500

FREE

Having paid the balance of your holiday 10 weeks prior to travelling, your **FRE HOLIDAY SPENDING MONEY** will be sent to you with your tickets in the form a cheque from the Holiday Club approximately 7-10 days before departure.

We reserve the right to decline any booking at our discretion. All holidays are subject to availability and the terms and conditions of the tour operators.

HOW TO BOOK

1. CHOOSE YOUR HOLIDAY from one of the major holiday companies brochures, making a note of the flight and hotel codes.

2. PHONE IT THROUGH* with your credit card details for the deposit and insurance premium, or full payment if within 10 weeks of departure and quote P&M Ref: H&C/MBC185. Your holiday must be booked with the Holiday Club before 30.6.92 and taken before 31.12.93.

3. SEND THE BOOKING FORM from the brochure to the address above, marking the top right hand corner of the booking form with P&M Ref: H&C/MBC185.

If you prefer to book by post or wish to pay the deposit by cheque, omit stage 2 and simply mail your booking to us. We will contact you if your holiday is not available·

Send to: The Holiday Club
P O Box 155 Leicester LE1 9G
* Tel No. (0533) 513377
Mon – Fri 9 am – 8 pm, Sat 9 am – 4 pr
Sun and Bank Holidays 10 am – 4 pm

CONDITIONS OF OFFER

Most people like to take out holiday insurance to cover for loss of possessions injury. It is a condition of the offer that Page & Moy will arrange suitable insuranc for you – further details are available on request. In order to provide comprehensiv cover insurance will become payable upon confirmation of your holiday. The insuranc premium is not refundable on cancellation

Free Holiday Spending Money is not payabl if travel on the holiday does not take place

The Holiday Club is run by Page & Moy Ltc Britain's largest single location travel agen and a long standing member of ABTA.

N.B. Any contractual arrangements are between yourselves and the tour operators not Mills & Boon Ltd.

ABTA 99529 **Page & Moy** Ltd Reg No. 115114